THE
NOWHERE
MAN

To Sandra

All the very best

[signature]

IAN WILSON

PROLOGUE

The painting leant against an easel in the window, beckoning me inside as though it had a desperate need to reveal an unspoken message. I opened the gallery shop door, a bell alerting the assistant to my presence, and he looked at me and smiled, before asking if he could help. I told him I wanted to look closer at the painting in the window and he went straight to it, carefully lifting it from its stand before propping it up onto a shelf and stepping back.

"Beautiful, isn't it?" he said.

I nodded. I was mesmorised by its detail: an arched wooden bridge leading into a cluster of trees, mist hovering from the ground, and the ripple of gentle waves just visible on the water beneath the bridge.

"I can't tell you who painted it, I'm afraid," the assistant said, "as there's no signature, and it was left on the doorstep this morning, wrapped in brown paper."

I wasn't interested in the artist; I was too fascinated by the way the image was making me feel. It was like I could hear birds singing and felt cold air against my face, my feet felt wet almost, as though I was paddling in shallow water, and I could almost sense someone on the other side of the bridge as I tried hard to see if the painter had included a person, perhaps surrounded by the mist.

"Is it for sale?" I asked.

The assistant nodded. "Yes, but I haven't got a price for it yet. I could make some enquiries and take your number, if that would help?"

I didn't even know if I wanted to buy it; I just wanted to stare at it. My senses were heightened now, as the murmur of the assistant's voice faded into the background in favour of another voice.

"Sarah," it said, and I put my eyes closer to it, finally seeing the figure of a person I almost knew was there. "Sarah." It spoke again, and I smiled, knowing I'd heard that voice so many times before.

CHAPTER ONE:

A knock at the door woke Sarah from a deep sleep.

Prising her eyes open to reveal bright sunlight breaking in through a gap in the curtains, she lifted her head from the pillow and scanned the room. With a shift of her body weight, she gradually lifted herself onto her elbow and tilted her head to one side, unsure whether she'd actually heard the knock, or dreamt it.

She rubbed her eyes and ran her hands through her wild auburn hair as she laid her head back onto the pillow, narrowly missing the box of half-eaten pizza and garlic bread, the pungent scent of garlic causing her to reel back to the other side of the bed. A constant rhythmic beat inside her head made her think that maybe a night out with the ladies wasn't a great idea after all.

Seconds passed before there was another knock on the door, slightly harder than the first.

Straining to see through her half open eyes, she glanced up at the clock: 9.30am; Sunday. Nobody ever knocked on Sunday mornings.

Forcing herself from the warmth of her duvet, she shuffled her way down the hall towards the door, and as she approached, she could make out the uniform of a police officer through the frosted glass window. Thoughts began running through her mind: what had she done last night? Surely it couldn't have been bad enough to warrant a visit from the police?

Tentatively, Sarah opened the door, squinting through heavy eyelids.

"Sorry to wake you ma'am, are you Sarah Pennington?" The male officer spoke first.

"Er, yes, why?"

The female officer then stepped forward. "Hi, Sarah, I'm Officer Julie Connor and this is my colleague, David Collins," she said, as they both showed Sarah their warrant cards. "I'm afraid we have some bad news about your father; he's been in an accident."

Sarah's eyes widened and her breathing became shallower. "What kind of accident? is he okay?"

Connor lowered her head and with a softness in her voice told Sarah that sadly, despite the best efforts of the paramedics, he had died.

Sarah was silent for a few seconds, lifting her head, averting her eyes from one officer to the other. She snatched in a deep gulp of air, lifted her hands to her face and covered her mouth as if trying to prevent a scream; her hands shaking uncontrollably, she began to reel back down the hallway, letting out a cry from deep within her.

Holding on to the spindles of the bannister she slid down the wall, landing heavily on the glossy, wood panelled floor, feeling the coldness of the floor against her thigh as she slowly curled herself into a ball, shaking and sobbing.

Connor put her arms around Sarah and helped her to her feet.

"I can stay with you for a while if you want. Would you like me to make you a cuppa?"

Sarah slumped into the chair at the table, wrapping her arms tightly around herself and rocking back and forth, tears streaming down her cheeks. It was a few minutes before she managed to speak. "I spoke to him on Friday, he was really looking forward to his fishing trip. What happened?"

"We're not sure of the details yet, but from what we've ascertained from witness statements, it looks like a tragic accident. Your father drowned in the lake where they were fishing."

"Drowned?" Sarah queried.

"It looks that way," Connor replied, a quick glance at Collins before she continued. "But, like I say, we will get more details in due course. Were you close to him?"

Sarah thought about that for a moment, the shock overwhelming her attractive features as she pictured him in her mind. "I always thought my dad was invincible, he was such a huge part of my childhood and always made time for me, even when he was busy."

Connor smiled and nodded. "Tell me about him," she offered, her family liaison skills focusing on Sarah's need to process what she'd just learned.

Her eyes darting around the room, Sarah rested them on a photograph. "Whenever I'd been bullied at school because of the colour of my hair, my freckles, or my white complexion, he'd make me stand up for myself, which built my confidence and probably made me the stubborn sod I am today." A little smile appeared through the tears and her eyes lowered as the memories flooded back and filled her head. "He'd tell me every day that I was unique with my bright red hair and green eyes. *'Emeralds on a white sandy beach in a sea of red, where others have a plain face'.* That was what he used to say; it was his way of making me feel special."

Connor responded with another smile and said, "That's a lovely description, he obviously had a way with words."

"Yes, he did. He had sayings for everything. When the bullies were getting me down, he'd say *'It's nice to be important, but it's more important to be nice'*, or he'd say, *'show them that you can dance in the rain'*."

She'd adored him, it was clear to see, and Connor just listened intently to whatever Sarah had to say, making a conscious effort not to interrupt.

She began to sob again, and a silence filled the room. Connor took the opportunity to ask her whether she was the only child, or did she have siblings, who she needed to contact.

"My parents had a son when I was six, but he died," she said. "He was born very weak and died when he was a few days old; we called him Julian. They were devastated, of course, and went through many stages of grief, but eventually they learned how to live with it, and never really mentioned it much afterwards. But I knew they always had him in their hearts."

Connor found herself struggling to hold back her own tears. "What about your mum; can we contact her for you?"

Sarah looked at her and half smiled through her tears. "You're not having much luck, are you? My mum died two years ago, there's only me and Dad; sorry, there *was* only me and Dad left."

Connor took a deep breath. "I'm so sorry, I should have guessed with you being next of kin. What was I thinking?"

"Not your fault, you weren't to know. She had a good life with my dad and when her time came, she went without suffering." A small smile escaped her lips as she continued. "I got my red hair and short temper from my mum; a five-foot-two pocket powerhouse. She was fiery, met my dad on a trip to Blackpool when she was eighteen. Within a few months they were married and lived on the farm in Stokley."

Connor pointed to a photograph on the fireplace. "Is that your mum? She's lovely, you look a lot like her." Sarah nodded, her sad expression prompting the officer to touch her arm. "You can talk to me, Sarah," she said. "It helps to talk in these situations."

It was an hour later when Sarah felt slightly better and Julie Connor once again touched her arm gently, announcing that she and her colleague needed to get back to work. "Will you be okay," she asked.

"I'll be fine, thank you, officer. You've been very kind."

"You can call me Julie; I'm sure we'll see each other again once the witness statements have been read and we have some more details for you." She stood up, then, "Now, get some rest and I'll be in touch very soon."

Sarah smiled and led the officers to the front door, assuring Julie she would try and rest, thanking her for spending time listening.

Once the door closed Sarah leaned back against it and slowly lowered herself to the floor. Sitting down and folding her arms around her raised knees she began to sob, tears running down her face, dripping off her cheeks and onto her thighs.

She was now completely alone, having lost her mother just two years earlier; her dad was her world and now he was gone, too.

What do I do now? Who do I need to speak to? Will the police have told Auntie Karen?

It dawned on her then, that there would probably need to be an autopsy, as thoughts of her dad being mutilated filled her head. With those thoughts burrowing into her mind, she pounded her fists into the door mat, then suddenly let out a loud scream and shouted, "WHY! If there is a God, then why take everyone from me? What am I supposed to do now?"

Gathering herself together she took her phone from her dressing gown pocket to call Auntie Karen, her dad's younger sister. Tears streaming down her face and settling onto the screen of her mobile, like raindrops on a tiny glass top table, she struggled for a few moments to dial the number, unable to stop her hands from shaking.

After a couple of rings Colin answered. "Hi Colin, is Auntie Karen there?"

"Hello, Sarah. Is everything okay? You don't sound too good."

"Er, not really, could I speak with Auntie Karen, please?"

A few moments later Karen came to the phone. "Hiya, love, is everything okay? Col said you sounded upset."

"Well, I've just had the police here. Dad's had an accident."

The phone was silent for a few moments and then Karen spoke, hesitantly, asking if he was alright.

Doing her utmost to fight back the tears, Sarah managed to force the words out through her ever-tightening vocal cords. "He's gone. He isn't coming back. What am I supposed to do now?"

"Oh, my dear God, what happened? Where is he now?"

Sarah broke down again, her voice trembling, as she told Karen she didn't know much, and just that he'd drowned while he was on a fishing trip and she would be heading back to the farm to organise things for the funeral.

"Me and Colin will travel down in the morning and meet you there," Karen told her. "You shouldn't be alone right now."

After ending the call, Sarah slumped back into the chair, reminiscing about when she'd decided it was time to be an independent lady and had moved into her own place. If she hadn't moved out, maybe her dad wouldn't have gone on the trip. He probably went because he was lonely. Was it all her fault? Did her dad die because she was selfish?

Forcing herself forward in her seat, she shook her head, and told herself to get those thoughts out of her mind. Then marched herself through to the bedroom to get her things together for her journey back to the farm.

CHAPTER TWO:

Driving to Stokley, Sarah went through the full plethora of emotions. As thoughts entered her head, she would cry, smile, and sometimes get angry to the point where she would punch the steering wheel as a release mechanism. Other drivers must have thought she was a bit simple, if they saw her beating up her own car, with tears in her eyes and a smile on her face.

Her childhood home, Pennington Farm, was located on the outskirts of a beautiful little village in Cheshire called Stokley. The whole village comprised of a few hundred houses, a few shops, a couple of pubs, which doubled up as restaurants, an old traditional post office, a small art gallery, and a stunning church at its centre built with light grey, almost white stone. Sarah had always loved the way it looked when it rained. The grey would darken to anthracite, and the stone would glisten, making a wonderful burnished surround to the stained-glass windows. As a child she'd always pretend it was an enchanted castle and that a knight in shining armour would one day whisk her away.

Surrounding the village were miles of farmland as far as the eye could see, beautifully maintained by the local farmers and making a spectacular view from Pennington Farm as it stood proudly positioned on the hill above the village.

Arriving at the farm, Sarah sat in her car for a few minutes contemplating whether to go in or find a room at one of the pubs for the night and wait for her auntie to arrive the following day.

After ten minutes staring at the door and pondering her options, her decision was finally made to go inside. After all, she would have to face it some time. Exiting the car, Sarah turned to look down the valley towards the village.

She'd forgotten how beautiful it was up there, looking down on God's country, with rolling fields containing multitudes of greens and yellows and the large oak tree in the distance where she'd spent many hours playing and climbing as a child.

Arriving at the front door, she was overwhelmed with a sense of anticipation, and trepidation, all at the same time. *The house is going to be empty.* She took a deep breath and nervously placed the key in the lock. At first it didn't move, then she remembered that she had to pull it back out slightly for the key to turn. Sarah smiled to herself at the thought that her dad never did get round to fixing it, despite years of promises to her mum.

Opening the door, a profusion of wonderful thoughts from her childhood came flooding back: the smell of her mum's baking filling the house when she came home from school, her mum shouting her to come in from the garden for freshly made potato cakes and crumpets, with a thick layer of butter from the local farms. Echoes of her dad cutting the grass and whistling tunes by his beloved Elvis permeated through her head.

He always whistled when he worked and he'd try to get Sarah to join in, but she never could get the hang of it; she could only conjure up a weird blowing noise and subsequently spit all over her chin.

She stepped inside and closed the door behind her. The house had been empty for a few days and was bitterly cold. Shivering, she pulled her cardigan around her shoulders, before making her way to the fireplace to see whether there were any logs in the scuttle to light the fire. There were a few, and neatly laid beside them were the firelighters and kindling.

Safe in the knowledge that her dad would have a stock in the log shed, she prepared the fire and had flames flickering within a few minutes. Her dad had taught her how to light a fire at the tender age of ten, despite the protestations of her mum who didn't like her doing it, saying that she was too young, and it was dangerous. Her dad would give her a cheeky smile and a wink, and show her anyway.

Once the fire was lit, she went outside to collect some logs from the shed. Collecting enough to see her through for the evening she closed the shed door behind her, its hinges rusting and stiff, and as she pushed against them, they made a sound like Chewbacca's growl as she forced the door closed. That made her smile again, another thing her dad had said for years that he was going to sort out, but never did. A quick spray of oil would probably have fixed it, but she always thought he quite liked it and that's why he'd left it.

After piling the logs at the side of the fire, Sarah took her things up to her bedroom, which was situated at the front of the house. Her mum and dad preferred the room at the back of the house, away from the road, so she'd had the master bedroom from being a small child.

As she reached the top of the stairs, she had an uneasy feeling of scopaesthesia, like she was being watched or someone was in the house. Sarah's room was directly ahead at the top of the stairs, whilst to the right, on an L shaped landing, the spare bedroom, bathroom, and her mum and dad's room were located.

Looking towards her mum and dad's bedroom she paused for a few seconds without breathing, listening for any sounds. Questioning herself and shaking her head she continued along the landing to her room. As she walked, the creaking floorboards made her stop for a moment as another memory of her childhood made her give a little chuckle to herself, thinking back to her sneaky trips downstairs to raid the fridge and then as a teenager, her tiptoeing along the hall when she arrived home late, hoping she didn't wake her parents.

As she opened the door to her room, she heard another door click closed. The hairs on the back of her neck stood up and a cold shiver ran through her. Her senses were on high alert now. *Is there someone in the house? Has Auntie Karen already arrived?*

"HELLO! Auntie Karen, is that you?"

No answer, so she shouted again, slightly louder this time. "AUNTIE KAREN!"

Sarah gently placed her bags on the carpet and turned slowly, edging her way along the landing until she reached the corner, cautiously leaning forward to gain a view towards the other rooms.

"COLIN!... AUNTIE KAREN! Is there anybody here?"

Again, there was no response. She virtually levitated along the landing now, to stay as quiet as possible. Upon reaching the first door, which was the bathroom, her body was shaking with the sensation of icy cold pins and needles on the backs of her forearms. She gripped the handle. Pushing it down as slowly as possible, she gently opened the door, and with her heart racing, eased her way inside, scanning the room with her eyes wide, not daring to blink. The room was quite small and had a distinct lack of hiding places, so it was obvious it was empty.

Backing out of the bathroom as slowly as she'd entered, she hesitantly edged her way out into the corridor again.

The room adjacent to the bathroom was the guest bedroom, which was rarely used for guests, and was mainly filled with junk when she'd lived there.

Sarah anxiously placed her hand around the handle, ensuring she had a good enough grip to pull it closed if there was anyone inside. She turned it; it stiffened as it rotated and with the extra pressure, it made a clicking sound before rotating further. She attempted to open the door but there was a pressure pushing it closed.

"WHO'S THERE!" she shouted.

She placed her shoulder against it and pushed harder, and with the extra effort the door opened and a chill hit her face that momentarily took her breath; the room was much colder than the landing. Edging her way in while keeping a tight grip on the handle, she noticed that the window was open slightly. Had someone broken in? Cautiously, she entered the room, her eyes scouring every corner. As she released the handle, the door slammed shut behind her with an unimaginably loud thud.

She let out a high-pitched scream and spun around, her heart pounding and her eyes wide open, and she drew in a deep breath and pirouetted around again to face the window. Expecting to be grabbed or struck by an intruder, her body tensed, and a tingling sensation wrapped around her shoulders causing her to shiver intensely, as she anticipated the attack; then, she realised, the culprit was a natural phenomenon.

"The bloody wind," she said, relieved, but at the same time annoyed with herself for being such a wimp!

Once her heart rate had dropped and she'd stopped shaking, Sarah closed the window and paused for a minute to look out at the garden, thinking how it needed some tender loving care to bring it back to her dad's standard.

As a child she'd spent hours staring out of that window, looking over the fields at the woodland behind the house, making up stories and poems that she saved in a scrap book. Her favourite time of year was when the bluebells filled the woodland and she recalled the poem she wrote about the naughty goblin:

A fairy hops, one hop, two hops and then she stops.
She sees a goblin break a bluebell
and scuttles off, the elves to tell.
The elves they hurry but all they found
was a sad little bluebell without its sound.
They searched the forest top to toe
But nothing for their efforts they have to show.
Suddenly a joyous shout of glee
The clapper is found in the bow of a tree.
The elves and the fairy dance and sing
While the bluebells play music ring-a-ding ding

Impressed with herself, she turned, gave another quick glance around and went back to her room to unpack.

After putting on her pyjamas, she went down to the living room, looking around at the old oak furniture that her mum used to meticulously polish every Sunday, when suddenly, she remembered that her dad had kept a photo album in the draw of the coffee table for years. Sarah opened the draw and took it out before settling down on the rug in front of the fire with a cup of tea.

The first page contained a black and white photograph of her mum and dad when they were young. Her mum looked so beautiful, wearing a short, checked dress that flared out at the bottom, a string of pearls around her neck and her hair up in a bouffant style. Her dad was dressed like a teddy boy with a massive quiff. He was a very handsome man in his youth, dark brown hair and striking blue eyes.

Below the photograph, written in faded ink, were the words, *Gareth and Carol, Floral Hall 1968.*

As she turned the pages, the memories came flooding back. Every picture told a story, and every story was a happy one. A few pages in there was a picture of Sarah in her father's arms, partially wrapped in a white shawl with a lemon cardigan and a glistening diamante-adorned dress. The caption beneath the photograph read *Dear Sarah, aged 8 months.*

Continuing through the album, Sarah began to feel moisture on the photographs and as she turned a few more pages she discovered they were getting wetter. Not just damp, but sopping wet. Like the album had been dipped in water.

She checked in the drawer, but it was bone dry. *Where has the water come from?* She scoured the ceiling for evidence of a leak and checked the table for any stain marks. Nothing. It was a mystery. No reason for the water, but a soaking wet book?

Maybe her dad had spilled a drink and hadn't realised that it had seeped into the drawer? Spreading the pages out and placing pieces of kitchen roll between them to stop them sticking together, she put the album in front of the fire to dry it out.

It was getting late and the sun was making its descent over the fields, leaving an orange glow against the twilight sky, and she remembered her dad putting a blanket over her while she curled up on the couch facing the window, with a mug of hot chocolate and freshly buttered crumpets that her mum had made. The whole sky would turn to shades of red, orange, yellow and purple as the sun settled down between the hills, and she recalled how much she'd loved to watch the array of colours in the sky. The view never ceased to amaze her. It would always be one of her fondest memories of her childhood at the farm.

CHAPTER **THREE**:

The next day Sarah had to attend Stokley police station to collect her dad's belongings. Something that she was dreading but, she knew, had to be done.

She woke early to the sound of birdsong and the rustling of the trees. It was so peaceful at the farm, hardly any man-made noise except for the odd passing car. After a light breakfast in the garden, she spent an hour pottering around and weeding before driving down into the village.

Stokley was only a small place so she was quite sure everyone would know about her dad by now, most of them knowing what had actually happened while others would make it up; typical of the village folk.

Sarah pulled into the car park at the rear of the police station and managed to enter without encountering any of the locals, which was a feat in itself, then approached the front desk. "My name is Sarah Pennington," she said to the desk constable.

"I know who you are," he replied with a smirk, "my mum used to babysit you when you were little. Don't you recognise me?"

"No, sorry. I'm not too good with faces."

"Terry. Terry Sutton. From Beechwood Grove. PC Terry Sutton now."

Sarah had no idea who he was and asked if he'd just be kind enough to bring her dad's belongings.

"No problem, Miss Pennington, I'll get them right away."

Terry scuppered off and quickly returned with a small box that he placed on the desk. "That's everything he had with him at the time."

She glanced down at it, thinking how insignificant it looked. Hardly anything in there, yet they were the last things her dad had touched. Looking up at Terry, she murmured, "Thank you. I appreciate your help."

She had another quick look through the items and asked whether they'd recovered a mobile phone. "It's odd that it isn't here, he always carried it."

"Sorry, the only things recovered are here," he assured her. Then, "Have you been to formally identify your father's body yet?"

Shocked at the question, Sarah replied, "Well, no. I haven't been told that I have to."

"Sorry, Miss Pennington, it's a requirement that somebody identifies him. I can run you down to the morgue now if you want?"

"Can't someone else do it?" Sarah asked. "Everyone in the village knew him, anyone could tell you it's him."

"I'm sorry, but it has to be a family member."

Reluctantly, Sarah agreed to do the identification and allowed Terry to lead her to a police car which he then drove a few miles to the morgue. Upon arriving, she was asked to wait in a small room while they prepared the body and then left her on her own to contemplate what to expect.

She'd never seen a dead person before, other than her mum, who'd looked really peaceful in her coffin at the funeral parlour and when Terry came back to the room and asked her to follow him, she looked up with tears in her eyes. He opened the door, expecting her to be behind him, but she was still sitting in her seat, nervously rubbing her hands together, her feet pushed up on tiptoe and her legs shaking.

"I'm not sure I can do it; does he look peaceful?"

"You'll be fine, they make them look as good as possible for the iden-tification."

Sarah took a deep breath, let out a loud sigh and stood up, clutching her bag tightly to her chest. Rocking back and forth as if revving herself up to move, she said, "Come on then, let's do this."

Entering the morgue, she felt a cold chill and wrapped her arms tight-er around herself. Her dad was covered with a white cotton sheet. Terry led her over to the side of the trolley and put his hand on her shoulder. "Are you ready?"

She took a deep breath, gave him a sideways glance and said, "Is anyone ever ready when you ask that question?" before looking down at the sheet covering her dad's face. "I'm ready," she confirmed, eventually.

The mortician slowly pulled back the sheet to reveal Gareth's face. Sarah just stared at him for a few moments before tears began to well up in her eyes and slowly roll down her cheeks. She cried silently, but in her head she was screaming; her heart felt completely smashed in her chest, and she began to shake. Initially it was a slight shaking of her hands, then her shoulders and her head began an involuntary juddering motion, and her legs became weak.

Terry placed his arms around her waist to prevent her from falling, and his eyes glazed with tears as he witnessed the pain she was clearly feeling.

"That's him. That's my beautiful dad."

Placing her hand on his face, Sarah glanced up at the mortician. "His skin is so soft and he's so cold." She leaned forward to kiss his head, but the mortician stopped her.

"You will be able to do that once the body is released to the funeral home," he said.

With Terry's help, she managed to turn and walk away, stopping and glancing over her shoulder for one more look before heading for the door.

"Are you okay?" Terry asked as they got in the car.

Sarah nodded her head. "What caused the graze and bruising on his forehead?"

"The report says he has a slight graze and small contusion on his forehead, consistent with a minor knock to the head. Probably caused when he fell into the water. Possibly hit the boat, or something in the water as he fell."

"Were there any other injuries?"

"No. The autopsy report states accidental death by drowning."

Arriving back at the station Sarah thanked Terry for looking after her, before heading to the village shop to pick up some groceries. Even though she was still in shock at seeing her dad, reality took over as she felt the need to make lunch for Karen and Colin when they arrived.

While choosing a few items from the shelves, it was like a whisper reverberating through Sarah's mind, a low hissing sound and the words, *Sarah*, *Gareth* and *Pennington* being emitted into her head. *Strange.*

She reached the till and Mrs Pearson, the proprietor and local news feed said, "Terrible news about Mr Pennington, he was a lovely man. We didn't always see eye to eye, but he always looked after you and your mum."

"Thanks, Mrs Pearson," Sarah said, a smile just visible on her lips.

Mrs Pearson cleared her throat. "So, what actually happened? Is it true that he…"

Sarah stopped her in her tracks. "He drowned. There's no gossip, it was an accident, plain and simple. He drowned." And with that, Sarah left the old hens to gossip between themselves and strutted across the high street towards the café.

As soon as she walked through the door the room fell into an eerie silence. Everyone stopped what they were doing, and every head turned to look at her, like a herd of meerkats with their necks stretched over each other and their ears pricked back listening for a predator. Except these 'meerkats' were listening for gossip.

She ordered a coffee and took a seat by the window.

Slowly, but surely, the whispering sounds started again. *Pss pss pss Pennington, pss pss pss Sarah.*

Julia Pearson placed Sarah's coffee on the table. "How are you holding up, love?"

"I'm fine thanks, Julia. Just need a bit of me-time, but not alone at the farm. Too many memories there. I might take a break once everything is sorted out."

"That's good," Julia said, patting Sarah's arm. "It's on the house, love," then scurried back to the counter where another customer was waiting to be served.

While she was in the café, Sarah received a text from Auntie Karen:

Be with you in half an hour

She finished her coffee quickly and made her way back to the farm where she prepared some sandwiches and made up the bed in the spare room. Staying in her mum and dad's room just didn't seem right and they probably wouldn't want to anyway.

Just as she'd finished making up the bed, there was a knock at the door. Sarah bounded down the stairs, skipping every second step, and snatched open the door to see her auntie standing there. She threw her arms around Karen and burst into tears.

"I had to identify him earlier, it was horrible. His skin was soft and silky, I expected it to be rigid. I can't get the image out of my head."

Karen pulled her close. "They should have waited for us to arrive and we would have identified him," she said, stroking Sarah's hair affectionately.

When they finally pulled away from each other, Sarah led Karen into the kitchen where she'd laid out a small buffet-style lunch, and then switched the kettle on. "Tea or coffee?"

Karen checked her watch. "It's twelve-fifteen, shall we have a glass of wine with our lunch, Col?"

The moment she heard that, Sarah remembered the last time they'd visited. Her dad had had a huge argument with Karen over her drinking and after they'd left, he labelled them as alcoholics and vowed never to have them at the house again.

"Erm. I'll have a tea, there's wine in the fridge if you'd prefer that, but I have to go to the funeral directors later and I need to inform the bank of dad's death."

Karen told Colin to get the wine from the fridge. "We'll just have a glass and then we can go to sort things out with Sarah."

Karen and Colin polished off a bottle and half of wine during lunch and as it began to take effect, Colin asked whether Gareth had life insurance and whether the insurance was up to date.

Sarah shrugged her shoulders. "It isn't something I've thought about yet, but I'll look into that once everything is sorted and dad's funeral is over," she said.

Colin stood up. "I'll go and check through his papers to see if I can find it."

Sarah gave him a glare that could burn through trees. "You will not!"she said, her voice raised. "That's dad's private stuff. I'll sort it out when I feel up to it."

Angry at Colin now, Sarah took flight up the stairs, went to her dad's bedroom door, and locked it. Then she took the key through to her room and hid it away in her childhood hiding place, behind a loose piece of skirting, down the side of her bed. The same place she'd kept her diary and any trinkets when she was a child.

Colin had managed to push every one of her buttons with that comment. Although she may only be a slight build and have a sheepish demeanour about her, when the redhead in her was ignited she could go off like a two-bob rocket!

Her dad used to wind her up and then shout, "STAND BACK! We have lift off." Then he'd laugh, which made her even worse.

Five minutes after the tantrum, her dad would take her down to the village for ice cream. So, it wasn't all bad being teased by him and she knew he never meant it.

Sarah stepped back into the kitchen to find Karen alone. "Sorry about that, love," Karen began, "he just doesn't put his brain in gear before opening his mouth."

"Where is he?"

Karen gestured towards the back door. "He's out there, I've told him he's better out of the way after that. You always could be a fiery little one, eh!"

Sarah noticed that the second bottle was empty. "I'll go down to the bank myself, you two need to get some sleep; you must be tired after that journey. I'll wake you when I get back and we can nip down to the Lion's Head for an evening meal. I'll book it while I'm out."

It was a twenty-minute drive to Curtis Funeral Directors, through country lanes to the next village. On the way Sarah pulled over into a lay-by, feeling she needed a break from the world for a few minutes. Settling back in her seat she pondered the decision to ask Karen and Colin to come down, knowing that, if anything, they'd added to her stress.

The setting that surrounded her as she sat in her car, was both beautiful and peaceful; the sound of the birdsong and the rustle of the wind through the fields around her was so soothing, it was almost hypnotic.

Continuing her drive along the country lane, she became aware that there was a slight mist in the air. She'd never noticed a mid-afternoon mist before, and her body shivered as she felt the temperature in the car lower suddenly: it was extremely cold. Turning a slight bend, she made out the shape of a person in the road. The mist had thickened to a dense fog, and she was travelling much too fast to stop. As she hurtled closer, the figure turned to look at her, but made no attempt to move, or even brace for the impact.

Pressing her foot hard onto the brake, she let go of the wheel and lifted her arms up to cover her face, screaming through gritted teeth, anticipating the thud as the car would surely hit the person in the road.

The impending collision made her jerk forward in her seat, causing the seat belt to hitch and her to stop suddenly as her body propelled forward. It was a split second of shear panic before she realised she was still in the layby.

The shock made her take in a deep breath and place her hands onto the wheel, whilst at the same time feeling a shuddering sensation travel through her entire body. It took a couple of seconds to gather her thoughts, until she realised she'd obviously nodded off for a minute or two.

After a few moments to calm herself down, she continued with the journey, arriving at the funeral directors shortly after.

"Hi. I've got a meeting with Mr Curtis about Gareth Pennington's funeral arrangements," she said to the lady at the desk as she walked inside.

Mr Curtis was a tall, thin man, obviously balding but trying hard to hide it under a messy comb-over, and wore a smart black suit and grey cravat. He was very compassionate and made Sarah feel totally relaxed through the whole process. The meeting didn't last long; her dad had already expressed his wishes to her after her mum died. Although it seemed a bit morbid at the time, Sarah was happy that they'd spoken about it, otherwise she'd be guessing what he'd want.

His wish was to be buried with her mum at St. Jude's Church in Stokley. He didn't want lots of flowers, he saw those as a waste of money, and he'd chosen the music he wanted to be played at the church. Other than that, Sarah was free to choose all other details.

After her meeting with Mr Curtis, Sarah called into the bank to inform them of his death and deliver a copy of the death certificate, then called at the Lion's Head to book the evening meal, although she wasn't sure she wanted to go now, following the afternoon she'd had with Colin.

CHAPTER **FOUR**:

The next few days with Karen and Colin were extremely tense. Niceties were passed but there was an unhealthy atmosphere that resulted in Sarah going out or spending time in her room as much as possible.

Colin hinted on a few occasions about Gareth's will, which caused Sarah to dislike him even more. Karen just lazed around in the kitchen, or out in the garden with a wine glass glued to her hand, drinking until she eventually passed out. At one point, Sarah contemplated getting her a teat to put onto the bottle, or setting up an intravenous drip, to save her cleaning the glasses.

On the third day, Sarah got up early and made them breakfast, calling upstairs to tell them to come down. Once they were seated, she announced that she thought it would be an idea if they were to head home.

"The funeral isn't until next week," she pointed out, "and you'll only be doing the same here as you would be at home."

Karen rolled her eyes. "Throwing us out of my brother's house, are you?"

"Not exactly," Sarah replied. "I'm asking you to go home, as this is my dad's house."

Colin made a short snorting sound as if starting to laugh. "We'll see about that when the will is read."

He'd gone too far; lit the blue touch paper and the two-bob rocket was well and truly set off.

Sarah stood up, her face puce with rage. "GET OUT, PACK YOUR STUFF AND PISS OFF!" she shouted. "I'm going out for an hour, and if you're still here when I get back, I'll have the police here and you'll be physically removed by them, followed by a swift kick up your arse with my size five boot."

Sarah grabbed her coat and charged out of the back door, slamming it hard behind her. As soon as she reached her car it dawned on her that her keys were still inside. Not wanting to go back in for them, she set off down the hill toward the village on foot, cursing and swearing with every breath, that she'd invited Karen and Colin to the house.

Just before the village was a beautiful little park with a few benches, a quiet zone, mainly used by the old folks, but also somewhere Sarah played as a child.

She collapsed onto one of the benches and folded her arms, huffing and puffing, before she leaned forward, her head clasped in her hands, and began to cry, more with anger, than anything else.

A man on the next bench looked over at her. "Is there anything I can do?"

She acknowledged him with a slight shake of the head. "Thank you, but I'd rather be left alone," she said.

"Okay, if you need anything, I'm just over here," he said.

After twenty minutes or so of grinding her teeth and clenching her fists as she thought of the sheer audacity of Colin, Sarah set off back to the house. As she left, she passed the man who'd spoken to her. He was sketching a picture of the park. "That's really good. I'm impressed. I'd love to stay and chat, but I have things to deal with. See you again."

The man gave a polite nod. "Thank you," he said. "I hope everything works out okay." Then, as she began to walk away, he shouted after her, "It would be lovely to see you again."

Now a woman on a mission, she headed back up the hill, reaching the house with her mobile phone in hand, ready to call the police if she needed. Their car had gone but the front door was wide open. Panting and her heart racing, she entered the house cautiously, hoping for it to be empty but ready and willing for battle if it wasn't.

The living room was empty and the kitchen was clear, except for the pile of wine bottles on the table. Striding up the stairs to the spare room, she threw open the door and, to her relief, the room had been cleared.

Letting out a deep breath, she slumped down on the edge of the bed as she puffed out her cheeks and muttered, "I'm glad that's over."

Feeling like a huge weight had been lifted from her shoulders, she left the room and headed to her own room, but as she approached, she noticed her bedroom door was ajar. It was definitely closed when she'd left.

Opening the door revealed what can only be described as carnage. The drawers of her dressing table had been emptied onto the floor, the bedside cabinet drawers were open and some of the contents strewn across the bed, and her wardrobe doors were wide open.

Realising that they'd been looking for the key to her dad's room, she took a leap across her bed and checked the hiding place. It hadn't been disturbed; they hadn't got what they were looking for.

Sarah was so happy to be rid of them she didn't bother to call the police; she simply wrote a single word text and sent it to Karen:

GOODBYE

The day of the funeral arrived, and Sarah hadn't heard from Karen or Colin. Hopefully, they'd be too embarrassed to turn up.

The car carrying her dad's coffin pulled up at the house with a second car for Sarah. It was meant to be for Sarah, Karen, Colin, and their children, but now, Sarah was alone.

A large amount of people had gathered outside the house: local farmers, a few of Gareth's friends, and some of the villagers. All wishing her well and handing her sympathy cards as she made her way to the car.

Feeling like every ounce of energy had been completely sapped from her body, every step was an enormous effort. Her eyes were a deep red, and the skin of her nose had been rubbed raw with the use of her handkerchief. She didn't think it was possible to cry any more, but she was wrong. The tears just kept flowing, and her nose was stinging from the constant rubbing.

A gentleman in a long black jacket and top hat held the door open as she entered. The inside of the car seemed cavernous, and she felt lonelier than at any point since her dad had died. Sitting in the corner in such a big seat made her feel small and extremely vulnerable, she felt beaten, her mind mulling through what the day had to offer. The reality sinking further and further into her and draining her of her very existence.

The car stopped and the driver opened the door, beckoning Sarah to exit with an outstretched hand. He spoke softly. "Madam, we're all here for you, the villagers will help you to be strong." With that she slowly managed to drag herself from the seat and out in time to see her dad's coffin being rolled out from the back of the hearse. The sight pierced her eyes and travelled deep into her heart. She felt like she was going to pass out, her legs weak and body feeling heavy. Gripping tightly onto the driver's arm she gathered herself together and made her way along the path to the doors.

When she entered the church, Sarah saw Karen and Colin in the pews near to the front. It was no time to be angry, but she wished they'd stayed away.

The church was quite full. Sarah hadn't realised how many people knew her dad. It was a wonderful service and the vicar helped by lightening the mood with a few stories about Gareth, some that Sarah hadn't heard before.

When the end finally came, Elvis Presley belted out 'The Whistling Tune', which caused Sarah to fall apart completely, her body shaking uncontrollably as the tears flowed like a miniature waterfall down her face. Mrs Pearson edged along the pew and placed her arm around her. "Come on, love, he'll be happy now he's with your mum."

Sarah knew she was trying to help but she probably couldn't have said a worse thing. "I want them both to be happy, here with me," she blubbered out through her tears, gripping her handkerchief with clenched fists, and pulling it apart as her shoulders and hands shook. She wanted to curl up and shut out the world but knew she had to somehow summon up the strength to get through the rest of the day.

Following the service, her dad was taken to be laid to rest with her mum as he'd requested, in the church yard that Sarah had imagined as her castle when she was a child. She didn't want to go to the wake, but felt that she had to since so many people had turned out to pay their respects.

She'd organised the function room at the Lion's Head for the wake, with a buffet and an open bar for a few hours so that people could celebrate Gareth's life.

As soon as she arrived, Sarah spoke to Graham, the landlord, about Karen and Colin. "I don't begrudge them a drink, but they have a problem. Please keep your eye on them."

After two or three drinks she was ready for home, not really wanting to be there, and thought that people wouldn't notice her slipping off to the toilet before heading back up the hill.

Turning on the tap to wash her hands, she raised her head to look in the mirror; for a split second she thought she saw someone standing behind her. Pivoting swiftly to look over her shoulder, she scanned the room, but it was empty. Slowly, she turned back toward the mirror, her eyes fleeting between the door and the cubicles for any movement.

She continued washing, glancing up at the mirror every few seconds to reassure herself that she was alone. She turned off the tap and looked into the mirror again, and this time the figure was there for a moment longer. An icy chill ran down her spine as she quickly turned her head, firstly to the right and then to the left to make sure she had a clear escape to the door. Grabbing a few towels, she turned and made a bolt for the exit, all the time continuing to scan the room.

Still shaking from the experience, Sarah went to each table thanking people for turning up and making her apologies, before heading home.

The house seemed lonelier than ever when she got back. In a way, the funeral had made it official that he'd gone, as before that, he was still there in body. It hadn't hit home when she'd been to see him in the funeral parlour. Today meant that he'd gone in both body and soul.

She had a restless night's sleep after curling up on the settee with a glass of wine and her memories, knowing that the next morning she had to attend an appointment with the solicitor for the reading of the will. She had no idea what to expect, but just hoped that whatever happened Karen and Colin wouldn't make a fuss.

Arriving at the solicitor's office, Sarah was met by a well-dressed young man who took her details and guided her through to a small meeting room where an elderly gentleman was sitting behind a large, shiny, oak desk. She couldn't help but notice that the desk was extremely well organised, everything neatly stacked, and the pens were lined up perfectly in a neat row, with a highly polished gold name plate, which read, *Mr G L Fletcher.*

The man behind the desk raised his eyes above his glasses, which were perched on the end of his nose, and through his thick grey, bushy eyebrows he acknowledged her presence.

"Good morning, Miss Pennington. I'm Graham Fletcher. I hope you're well."

"I'm as well as can be expected in the circumstances, Mr Fletcher."

"Would you like tea or coffee?"

"No thank you, I'd just like to get this over with please."

Mr Fletcher checked his watch and looked up at the clock on the wall. "We're awaiting Mr and Mrs Langton. I believe they're your auntie and uncle."

"They were," Sarah replied, rolling her eyes.

While they waited Sarah sat cross-legged, her eyes scanning the room, which at first glance seemed to be quite well furnished with old wooden bookshelves, adorned with law books and neatly stacked foolscap files. Looking beyond the polished wood, the décor behind was shabby, the old woodchip wallpaper hanging loose in places and stained from many years of smoking. The carpet, which seemed to have once been a beautiful red and grey colour, now had threadbare areas peeping through the pile, leaving straw-coloured criss-cross strands of twill exposed.

Sarah's eyes eventually fixed on the old sash window, propped open with what looked like an antique glass ashtray adorned with a popular cigarette logo. The thick, off white, wooden window frame surrounded a misted glass, through which Sarah could see the dark clouds and fine rain that had started as she'd arrived.

A few seconds later there was a tap on the door and the young man who'd previously brought Sarah through, entered with Karen and Colin.

"Good morning, Mr and Mrs Langton," Graham Fletcher said in a friendly tone. "I'm Graham Fletcher. Thank you for attending. Please, take a seat." He gestured towards the remaining two chairs next to where Sarah sat.

"Morning, Your Honour," Karen responded, followed by a little bow of her head.

Mr Fletcher gave a little smile and nodded back, before he picked up the paperwork and shuffled it before clearing his throat and lowering his eyes to see through his carefully balanced glasses.

"We are here to read the last will and testament of Gareth James Pennington," he announced glancing at each of them in turn.

Karen interrupted. "Do you need our identification to prove he was my brother, your honour?"

"Please, call me Mr Fletcher, I'm not a judge. We can continue without the identification for now."

"Thank you, Your Honour."

With a roll of his eyes and a slight shake of his head, he continued to read through the legal jargon until he reached the section of bequeath.

"I, Gareth James Pennington, do bequeath ten thousand pounds to each of my nephews, Patrick and Scott Langton. All remaining estate, including Pennington Farm, any and all savings and all of my, and my wife's jewellery, I leave to my daughter, Sarah Louise Pennington."

Colin jumped up out of his seat. "That can't be it, what about his sister, surely he's seen her straight."

Karen turned to Sarah and snarled, "You will be hearing from my solicitor, young lady."

Sarah turned sideways on her seat to face Karen, then smiled at her. "I knew what my dad was doing with his money and I didn't agree with it. I was willing to give some of his estate to you, until you tried to steal from me. Now, you can rot in hell for all I care." She then swivelled back in her seat, stared at the old fireplace with her lips pursed and her eyes fixed, and finished with, "Goodbye and good riddance."

Mr Fletcher turned his head to try and hide the smile on his face, then turned to Karen. "I'm afraid, Mrs Langton, if you wish to pursue a share of the estate, it will take a considerably long time and a substantially large sum of money to do so." Then he stood up and put his glasses on the desk before adding, "Thank you again, for your attendance today. My secretary will see you out."

Karen and Colin stood up, both lost for words as they walked towards the door and opened it. Sarah half-expected them to say something else, but they left, leaving the door gaping open.

"How did you know what was in the will?" Mr Fletcher asked, sitting back down at his desk and reaching for his glasses.

"I had no idea," Sarah admitted, smiling, "but it felt great telling her that I did. I honestly thought he'd have shared it, but once I met them properly, I know why he didn't."

Mr Fletcher smiled. "You'd make a great lawyer with that poker face. Well played."

She blushed a little. "Thank you, Your Honour," she said, and bowed her head before giving him a huge smile.

Sarah left the solicitor's office and meandered slowly back towards her car, feeling a lot better than she did before she'd arrived. Her way home took her passed an art gallery, not something she was particularly interested in, mainly because she'd never had the finances to partake in such a hobby. She stopped for a few moments admiring the front of the building and its wonderful old structure, possibly a stable or part of a mill in a former life. Peering in through the window she noticed a sketch sitting on a small wooden easel.

I'm sure I've seen that somewhere before. Stepping into the gallery, she scanned the room to see whether she might know anyone who might accost her with questions about her dad and how she was feeling; something that she could do without right now. It seemed to be all clear, however, so she headed inside.

After strolling through the many sculptures, paintings and sketches, she asked a young assistant how much the sketch in the window was.

"Sixty pounds," the assistant replied. "It's a glorious sketch of the treescape in St. Theresa's park."

"Ahh. That's why I recognise it," Sarah said with a nod "I spent a lot of time in that park as a child. I knew I'd seen it before. I'll take it."

CHAPTER FIVE:

Much of Sarah's time over the coming eighteen months was spent travelling, mainly around Europe and the Greek islands; she hadn't enjoyed much travelling in her youth, her dad wasn't one for long trips, so a few days in Wales or Cornwall was his limit. Now that she could travel and had the finances to do it, the sky was the limit. After she'd visited most of the places that she'd always dreamt of seeing, she settled down in the farmhouse and began making plans for her future, the first being to integrate with the community, maybe join a reading group or a walking club.

It was a few days later while walking through the village that she decided to call into the art gallery. Not a big shop, but crammed nonetheless, with beautiful paintings and images of the local area, dotted around the walls on display, with small price tags hanging from their frames. One of her favourites was a painting of an old timber bridge that seemed to lead into a woodland, painted as if the artist was standing just before the bridge looking over into the trees beyond; a mist covered the woodland and she could just make out a footpath and what seemed like the figure of a man in the distance.

"Beautiful is an understatement." She turned at the voice, to see a stranger, standing behind her; a friendly smiling face, his dark brown, almost black hair pulled back tight into a ponytail, and his eyes a striking blue, which reminded her of her father.

He spoke again. "The painting you were looking at, it's beautiful. Don't you think?"

Sarah took a step back and looked him up and down. "I'm sorry. Do I know you?"

He smiled, took a few steps back and gave a slight shake of his head. "Technically, no," he said, apologetically, "but we did meet very briefly in the park a while ago. You were a little upset and I asked if I could help. You stopped for a second or two and commented on my sketch."

Sarah recalled the meeting, but she wouldn't have recognised him again if she'd fell over him in the street.

"Did we speak, at the time?"

"Briefly, like I said, you commented on my sketch."

"I assume it was a good comment, otherwise you wouldn't be speaking to me now."

"So good that you bought the sketch a few days later."

Sarah thought back to the day of the funeral when she'd called in to the gallery.

"I have it in my hallway, it's very impressive," she said. "I thought I recognised it, but I didn't connect it with seeing you. I assumed I recognised it because it was the park where I played as a child." She smiled at him. "It's nice to meet the artist."

"My name's Jonathon, I'm very pleased to meet you. You obviously have very good taste in art." He smiled then shuffled about on his feet, a little nervously. "I'd like to get to know you better over a coffee if that would be okay?"

Thinking he sounded a little keen, Sarah hesitated for a moment and looked around the gallery. There were plenty people around and she didn't think there'd be any harm in a quick coffee, so she nodded politely. "I'm Sarah," she said, holding out her hand. He shook it. "Coffee sounds good, thanks," she added, before turning back to look at the painting.

"I've seen you in the gallery before," he said. "You have a very good eye for a painting. Do you work in the art world, or maybe your husband is an artist?"

She turned back to him. "I've visited the gallery a couple of times when I've been home, and I don't have a husband."

"Boyfriend?"

"No. I don't have the time or the energy for a man in my life right now, Too messy and too much trouble." Turning her back again, she once more studied the painting as Jonathon moved to stand beside her. She stared at it for a few moments and then turned to him and said, "You can imagine yourself standing where the artist was when they painted this. I wonder where it is and who the person in the distance is? I like to make my own story up when I see a picture like this." Jonathon nodded and glanced at her before she continued. "I imagine this is a beautiful little village in Scotland and the bridge takes you into a lovely woodland, or a forest where there's an enchanting little cottage. Maybe the person in the distance is the owner of the cottage out for a stroll, and his wife is just ahead of him walking the dog, just too far to see her through the mist." He smiled, impressed by her imagination. "What do you see when you look at it," she asked, turning to face him again. "Do you imagine what the story behind these paintings are, or do you just see paintings?"

He stepped closer to the it and studied it for a minute. "I imagine the painting to be in the Lake District, far out from a town or village, deep within a forest, and the figure is a man with nowhere to go and nobody to see, he owns nothing and needs nothing, he's just a figure. I think he's 'The Nowhere Man'."

Unimpressed with his story, Sarah began to walk away, rolling her eyes and shaking her head.

"How about that coffee?" Jonathon asked.

"Yes, let's get a coffee before you reduce another painting to misery on canvas," she replied, glad to escape the gallery and not have to listen to his ridiculous stories of 'The Nowhere Man'

After the waitress had taken their orders, they sat in an awkward silence for a few minutes before Jonathon eventually gave out a little cough and said, "I take it you didn't like my theory about the painting?"

"No, I didn't," she said with a shrug. "It's a drab enough world without imagining people with nothing and nobody. You made that painting seem sad. Paintings should bring joy and colour into your life."

"I apologise if you didn't like what I said, but that is exactly what I saw when I painted it."

Sarah looked at him with doubt in her eyes. "You're telling me you painted that picture?"

"Yes. If you want to check, go back and look at the signature."

Jonathon picked up a napkin and signed it before handing it to Sarah, gesturing for her to go and look.

"I'll keep an eye on the drinks while you're away, just go and see for yourself."

Sarah made her way back to where the painting was hanging, and sure enough the signature was the same: *J Ripley*, the exact same signature that Jonathon had scrawled on the napkin.

She looked closer, her face almost touching the brush strokes, its colours vivid and drawing her in towards it. Beautiful greens and browns jumped out at her and she could almost see the trees moving in the breeze and the leaves swirling around as they were falling; in her mind, she could even hear the sound of the branches rustling and feel the cold of the moist fog on her face. And, bizarrely, as she stepped forward, she could feel the pine needles through her soft soled shoes.

Amazed by the clarity, she looked deeper into the painting until her eyes paused on a faint figure: a man, glancing over his shoulder. Sarah strained her eyes to get a clearer look, but no matter how much she tried, she couldn't see clearly through the mist. For one split second the figure looked directly at her, and to her horror it was almost featureless. She could make out faint lines but no face. She felt a cold chill creeping along her spine, her eyes afraid to blink, her ears locked into her surroundings, whilst her hands were clenched tight. She was half-expecting the figure to pounce after she lost sight of him in the thickening fog.

Sarah found herself drawn further and further into the forest in search of the mysterious figure, her feet cold and wet from the dew on the grass, then suddenly, she felt a pull on her arm and somebody calling her name. Her instinct was to scream, but then she realised she was back in the gallery as Jonathon was shaking her shoulders and repeating her name.

"Sarah, Sarah. Are you okay? You're as white as a ghost, come and get your coffee."

She gathered her thoughts and slowly began to walk back to the coffee shop, glancing back at the painting with every other step.

"Who is that in the painting?" she asked, as they sat down again and she took her coffee cup in her hand.

"It's really hard to explain. I call them 'Nowhere People', I see them whenever I paint. I've tried to speak to them, but I can't get their attention, they just stand there until my painting is done and then they're gone. It's like they were never there, but I know that they were."

"So, you imagine them, they're not real people?"

"They're real while I'm painting and then they go," Jonathon replied with a shrug. "I don't know whether they're real or a figment of my imagination but they're in all of my paintings."

Sarah slumped back in her seat and cupped her face in her hands, wondering what had just happened, how she'd felt like she was actually in the painting. The forest and the figure were so real; she glanced down at her feet and her shoes were wet. Her thoughts went back to when she'd entered the gallery and she wondered if there could have been a possibility that the ground was wet; that would explain it.

They finished their drinks and made their way to the exit, but just as they got outside, Sarah made an excuse of leaving something in the gallery and said goodbye to Jonathon.

He passed her a card. "That's my number," he said. "I'd really like to see you again, please give me a call."

"I will," she replied. "I just need to go back for my scarf, I left it in the coffee shop. I'll call you when I can."

Once back inside the gallery, she headed straight back to the painting and sought out a staff member.

"I'd like to buy this painting," she said, unable to tear her eyes from it.

"I'll bring the owner, he'll know better whether it's for sale or not."

A gentleman approached her, and with a European accent, said. "Hi. My name is Anton, I am the proprietor. I believe you would like to purchase a painting."

"This one on the wall," she said, pointing at it. "I believe it's by Jonathon Ripley."

Anton seemed a little unsure as to whether he wanted to sell the painting.

"Are you sure, madam? I have previously sold this painting and it has been returned. People say it is unlucky." He turned around and started to point out a few other images dotted around the gallery's walls. "Maybe you would like another painting. We have some beautiful images from local artists, would they be of interest?"

"No. I don't want another painting; I want this one. Is it for sale or not?"

"It's not cheap, madam, this painting is eight hundred pounds. I can't go any lower than that, so it isn't worth bartering with me. I'd also add that we wouldn't want to have it returned again. In other words, this painting is sold on a non-return basis."

"Okay, consider it sold. Can you deliver it to my address tomorrow?"

"Yes, madam." Then, "Are you sure you wish to take this one?"

"Yes, I'm certain. Please deliver it to Pennington Farm tomorrow."

CHAPTER SIX:

S arah made her way home through the village and out into the country roads, which headed towards the farm. The small farms with the
farmers out working the land reminded her of her childhood; days spent
on the tractor with her dad, her mum bringing freshly made bread and
soup out to the fields for her and her dad for lunch.

The farmhouse and the gardens at Pennington farm were beautiful,
and plenty enough work for Sarah. Six acres of land that her dad used to
work. As much as she treasured the memories, she'd never been interested in farming, so she'd arranged to lease the land off to other farmers in
the area to graze their sheep and cows on.

She arrived home just as the sun was setting, and put some logs on the
fire before settling down in the front room to watch the sunset. It was
always a pleasure to watch as it set between the hills opposite the house.
The myriad of colours in the sky never ceased to amaze her as she curled
up on the sofa, wrapped in an old checked blanket, with her book in her
hand and a glass of her favourite wine on the table beside her.

After a while, the room began to darken except for the glow of the
fire, which was also starting to dim as the logs burnt out leaving an orange glow around the room. Her eyes began to close as she tired, partially due to the wine and the heat from the dying embers, but also because
she'd lacked sleep following her flight home a few days earlier. As she
began to drop into a deeper sleep, she heard a scratching noise coming
from the kitchen.

Initially, Sarah dismissed the sound and pulled the blanket up higher
as if to comfort herself, nestling her head deeper into the pillow. But
breaking the silence came another scratching sound, slightly louder and
more persistent, which really grabbed her attention.

She sat bolt upright with a sharp intake of breath, eyes wide open, her body tensed with fear. Grabbing hold of the empty bottle from the coffee table, she whispered, "Who's there?"

No response. Then a tapping and more scratching. She stood up as quietly as possible, and shuffled her way slowly towards the kitchen, stopping with her back to the edge of the door. "Who's there?" This time, her voice was a bit louder and slightly more forceful. Hopefully, whoever it was, wouldn't hear the fear in her tone.

Placing her trembling hand onto the handle, she tentatively pushed open the door. Her hairs stood on end, she began to edge in, feeling frantically for the light switch, which was still too far away to reach. "WHO'S THERE!" she shouted,

Again, there was no answer, but was that a sound of someone breathing or was she hearing her own breathing echoing through the room? With her heart pounding in her chest, she made a jump for the light switch and held the wine bottle above her head. The light suddenly filled the room and with a quick scan she deduced that it was empty. Sarah edged her way over to the pantry; the door was slightly ajar. *Have I left the door open? Is someone hiding in there?* At this point her fear was palpable, and she could feel the damp coldness of her skin and the goose bumps raising the hairs on her arms. Her heart was racing, thumping rapidly in her chest.

Trembling with anticipation and with the wine bottle poised to strike, she seized the handle of the door. As she threw it open, she expanded her chest and snarled, making the angriest face she knew how to make.

The pantry had all the food and wine that she'd put in there but nothing that could have made the sound she'd heard. Glancing around the room, she began to breathe slower and her body began to relax. Until she heard the sound again: a tapping and then scratching, like a knife dragging across the plastic of the door. Was there somebody trying to get in? It was pitch-black outside, and the light inside made it impossible to see through the glass. Adversely, it would make it easier to see in from the garden, giving anyone outside the advantage of knowing Sarah's movements.

She shuffled her feet keeping her back to the kitchen cupboards, and made her way slowly around to the back door. Putting her hand on the light switch next to the door, she braced herself in anticipation of the horror that was going to face her when the light went out.

One, two, three. She flicked the switch and gave out an almighty scream. Reeling back, she snatched a deep breath to scream again, then stopped herself. Aided by the moonlight she realised the figure she thought she'd seen was her raincoat, the one she'd hung out to dry earlier that day. It was swinging against the door in the wind.

Her heart still beating fast, she opened the door and took the coat from the line.

"Fancy being terrified of my own washing. I won't hang it there again in a hurry," she said, as she walked back into the kitchen, still breathing heavily from her ordeal.

A little later, after she'd calmed down, she relaxed herself into the bath, sipping on a glass of wine, the warm water lapping over her naked body, as her thoughts went back to the gallery and the painting. Maybe Jonathon had purposely spoken to her to get her to buy it; he could have set her up and she'd fallen for it, hook, line, and sinker. She even started to think that Anton was probably in on it too, and him and Jonathon were rubbing their hands together with four hundred quid each in their pockets.

"I might ring up in the morning and cancel," she thought.

Her eyelids grew heavy as the soothing warmth of the water was beginning to make her feel drowsy causing her to eventually fall asleep.

She could see a figure, just like the one in Jonathon's painting. Similar to her experience in the gallery, she just couldn't make out any features, but the figure kept trying to get her to walk towards it. She felt like it was trying to draw her closer, but she was unable to move too near, as though it didn't want her to actually get there.

Looking down she realised she was walking through a stream; the water was completely still, not so much as a ripple around her legs as she waded through. It was getting deeper and deeper, passing her thighs. As she walked further in, it began to get colder, passing her chest and reaching her neck, cold enough to affect her breathing, and causing her to shiver uncontrollably, until it reached below her chin.

As she raised her head to keep above the surface, she was starting to panic and could feel herself beginning to sink into the mud at the bottom of the stream. It felt like her feet were set in concrete and it was taking her lower into the water.

Then the water rose above her chin and started to enter her mouth. Snatching for breath and spluttering, she started to thrash about trying to get her feet free. In her panic she grabbed a piece of driftwood and then heard a loud smashing sound, which made her open her eyes and sit forward.

Still in the bath, the water now ice cold,she tried to focus on her surroundings, before noticing the water was turning red. A thick red liquid ran down the side of the bath, diluting in the water, which prompted her to let out a muffled scream.

After a few panicked moments, however, she realised she'd dropped the wine glass onto the edge of the bath and cut her hand, the liquid in the bath being blood from the cut. Standing up she wrapped it with a flannel before drying herself and putting on her dressing gown.

It was only then that she realised the time: she'd only been the bath for fifteen minutes. How was the water so cold after such a short time?

CHAPTER **SEVEN**:

S arah was awakened the next morning by the sound of knocking on the front door; she put on her dressing gown and hurried down the stairs. A wiry-looking man stood on the step with her delivery of the painting, his deep sunken eyes and high cheek bones making her a little wary of him. She closed the door and propped her new purchase up on the dining table, eager to tear off the brown paper it was wrapped in. She made herself a cup of tea then went towards the table where she put the mug down. But just as she pulled out a chair to sit down, the painting somehow fell to the floor, lying faced down.

A gust of wind, perhaps? She looked around the room to see if she'd left a door open, but there was no draught and definitely no open doors or windows.

Sarah got up from the chair and picked the painting up, making sure that this time it was leaning far enough against the table that it couldn't fall over. Then, settling back into her seat, the painting fell over onto its face again, but this time there was a thud, which she thought seemed really loud considering the distance it had fallen.

A little hesitant to pick it up again, she lifted it from the floor and this time leant it against the table legs. The next question was where to hang it, and her first thought was above the fireplace. But that space was already taken by a beautiful picture of her mum and dad. There was a place, however, in the dining area above the table, which had a few random pictures of her as a child, of holidays they'd been on as a family, so she decided to take those down and put the painting there instead.

Finishing her tea, she went through to the kitchen, and just as she walked in, she heard a bang in the lounge. Rushing through, she was shocked to see the picture of her mum and dad resting on top of the fireplace, having obviously fallen off the wall. The picture had been up there for years, solid and secure. *How did that fall off?* She checked the back of it, along with the cord used to hang it up with, noticing it was still in perfect condition *Very odd.*

After putting it back and checking it was securely attached, she went back through into the kitchen to dry the dishes, and a few minutes later there was another bang. A little unsettled, she returned to the living room and sure enough the picture was off the wall again, and sitting sideways on top of the fireplace, only this time the frame was cracked, which meant it couldn't be rehung.

Sarah loved that picture; she was quite upset that it had been damaged, so decided to take it to the village and get it fixed. Wrapping the picture in newspaper to prevent any more damage she headed to the gallery to ask if it could be repaired.

When she arrived at the gallery Anton was there at the doors, just opening up.

"Did you receive the painting okay, madam?"

"Yes, I did. I haven't hung it yet because I need to remove some others before I do. I was just calling to see whether you could repair a frame for me. It's an old picture of my mum and dad. It fell off the wall twice this morning, which was a bit odd because it has been up there for years."

Anton took the picture and unwrapped it. "How far did it fall? The frame has split in two."

"It only fell a few inches; the damage can't be all that bad"

"Madam, this frame is completely split in two, it must have fallen at least ten feet for that to happen. It'll take me a week or so to get the new wood to replace it. Sorry."

Sarah was baffled by his comments. "Let me see, there was hardly any damage when I put it in the car, and I made sure it didn't move all the way here, it was on the front seat, right at the side of me."

She looked at the frame, and just like Anton had said, it was completely split in two. "That's just not possible, I wouldn't have believed it if I hadn't seen it with my own eyes. I've got a replacement to put up while you repair it, so can you just get it back to me as soon as possible."

While in the village, she called in to a few shops and just happened to run into Jonathon. "Hi, Sarah, how are you?"

"I'm a little bit upset, actually," she began. "A picture of my mother and father fell off the wall this morning and it's damaged. It's been there for years and just fell off. I can't understand how it happened."

"That's awful, can it be repaired?"

Sarah nodded. "Yes, I've dropped it into the gallery; Anton's going to fix it. I'll replace it for now with the painting I bought yesterday."

"Painting?"

"I went back into the gallery after meeting you yesterday and bought your painting. The one with 'The Nowhere Man'."

Jonathon was silent for a few seconds, then, "Where is the painting now?" he asked.

"It's at home, why?" she replied, a little taken aback by his question.

He seemed a little shaken, and looked at the bandage on her hand. "What happened?"

"It was my own stupid fault, I fell asleep with a glass of wine and the glass fell over and smashed, cutting my hand."

"Ouch, painful." Jonathon smiled briefly. "Did you keep my number?" he asked.

"I did," she said, not wanting to get into a conversation about them meeting up again. "Anyway, I must get on, stuff to do, people to see..."

Jonathon nodded, getting the hint. "Hope to see you soon," he said, as she left the shop with a bag of groceries.

It was late afternoon when she arrived back at the house, feeling a chill in the air as she entered through the front door. She lit the fire, put the groceries away, then made some tea.

"Hanging the new painting can wait until tomorrow. I think I'll have a chilled night and listen to some music," she said to no one in particular. And with that thought in mind, she headed off to get changed into her favourite pyjamas and slipped on her dressing gown, before taking her usual place on the sofa and turning the radio on to listen to her most loved music. As she did most nights, Sarah watched as the sun went down and the sky went through its dazzling array of colour.

The ten o'clock news came on the radio and then the presenter started to play one of Gareth's favourite songs and she closed her eyes, imagining her Dad singing at the top of his voice, while he was working in the garden. He had a lovely voice but would only ever sing when he was gardening or in the shower. She'd tried to get him to sing in the local pub on karaoke, but he'd always been too shy.

The song was halfway through when she heard a faint voice, almost behind the music. At first, she struggled to make out what it was saying, but as her ears began to separate the song from the voice, she began to home in on what was being said: *"Help me!"*

Despite turning down the sound to try and hear the voice more clearly, all she could hear was the music. Her first thought was that it could be interference from another channel, so she lowered the sound again and listened intently, but to no avail.

Deciding instead to go to bed, she began her usual ritual of checking the windows and doors before heading up the stairs. But as she reached the top, she heard the voice again. *"Help me."*

It can't be the radio, it's been unplugged, she thought before going back to the living room to listen studiously for the voice again. Sitting in total silence for several minutes, there was nothing except the sound of the wind travelling through the chimney. She shook herself and stood up, making her way back to the stairs. *Maybe I need to leave the wine alone for a bit.*

CHAPTER **EIGHT**:

The following day, Sarah was sitting out on the lawn in the back garden, drinking in the fantastic view down the valley into the village. She loved to sit out on hot days and watch the world go by, or tend to the flowers and hanging baskets. The garden was filled with lavender and jasmine and on summer days, the scent of the flowers was beautiful. That, combined with the wonderful landscape surrounding her, made for a fantastic place to relax.

While she was sitting in her swing chair a car stopped at the side of the garden and a man got out of it then walked around to the driveway. She couldn't make out who it was at first, because of the hedgerow, but once he turned the corner, she realised it was Jonathon.

"Hi, Sarah, just thought I'd call in to see how your hand is and make sure everything is okay with you."

A bit shocked at his sudden unannounced visit, she said, "Jonathon. How did you find out where I live?"

"Anton, at the gallery, you gave him your address for the delivery."

"Ah right, good job it's not a secret, eh?"

"Beautiful house, and a lovely garden, I'm very impressed. How do you fancy nipping out into the village for a coffee?" he said, a beaming smile lighting up his face.

"I have coffee here. I can make you some if you'd like to join me?"

"Yes, that would be great, so long as you don't mind the intrusion."

She laughed. "Well, Jonathon, you seem to make a habit of intruding."

Disappearing into the house, Sarah made two coffees and took them back outside, placing them onto the wooden table. A bit of small-talk was exchanged while they sat in the sunshine admiring the views, and then Jonathon shuffled in his chair.

"Erm. Have you put the painting up yet?" he asked.

She shook her head. "Not yet. If it comes to that I could probably do with a hand putting it up, if you don't mind."

"Anything to help, after all you did buy my painting, so it's only fair that I help put it up, I suppose."

Sarah led Jonathon inside and took him into the living room where she slid the painting from behind the sofa. She unwrapped it and lifted it up to the light so they could get a good look at it.

"Is it as good as it looked in the gallery?" Jonathon asked.

"It's lovely. You know how to capture light and shades in your paintings. Maybe one day you could paint the view from my garden down to the village?"

"I'd be happy to," he replied.

Between them, they managed to get the painting up on the wall and straighten it up. Jonathon stepped back and studied it. "You haven't had any more dreams, have you?"

Sarah gave him a quizzical look. "No. I haven't had any dreams, why do you ask?"

"Just wondering, with you having the dream when you cut your hand."

"I haven't had a dream, but I have heard voices. Well, I think I have, though it may have been static over the radio."

"What voices?"

"It sounded like somebody whispering, but I couldn't be certain."

"What were they saying?"

Sarah shrugged. "It sounded like 'help me', but I couldn't be certain."

Jonathon looked deep into Sarah's eyes. "Sarah, like I've said before, if you need me, give me a call."

She smiled. "Thanks, but I'm okay."

"I really must go," he said, glancing at his watch. "Thanks for the coffee, and sorry to have just dropped in on you like that."

"It's not a problem, and you're welcome. And thanks for helping me hang the picture; I couldn't have done that on my own."

She saw him to the door and watched as he got into his car and drove away. As Sarah closed the door and walked back into the lounge, she stopped to look at the painting. It seemed bigger than she'd remembered and the colours were even more vibrant. It would take another hour in the garden to finish up and so she headed back out, and on her way, her mobile phone rang.

"Hi, it's me, Jonathon. Just wondering whether you fancy something to eat and a drink or two this evening?"

"I'm a bit of a mess," she said, thinking how keen he must be to see her again. "I've been working in the garden all day." She thought for a moment, then said, "If you want to give me an hour or so, I can make something here. You bring the wine and I'll cook something. How does that sound?"

"Fantastic, I'll be there for seven thirty."

"By the way, any wine except Pinot, it doesn't seem to agree with me at the minute," she added, before hanging up.

Seven thirty arrived and there was a knock at the door.

"Perfect timing, the food will be ready in ten minutes. Get some glasses out of the corner cupboard and settle yourself down at the table."

Jonathon did as instructed and Sarah brought through the starters. "Hope you like Minestrone soup. It's homemade."

"Sounds lovely, one of my favourites," he said.

Asking about his artwork, Jonathon was happy to tell her how he'd got started and how much he loved to paint. "I've only completed five paintings so far, but I have several others unfinished. Apart from yours, I have no idea where who bought the other four that were sold."

They finished the soup and Sarah moved the dishes, taking them into the kitchen before coming back to the table laden with two plates filled with delicious-looking food.

Jonathon took one look and said, "This looks wonderful Sarah; it's like you already knew the best meal to cook for me."

Sarah smiled and picked up her knife and fork. "It's just a chicken chasseur, nothing special really. I'm glad you like it, though."

After they'd finished, she noticed it was beginning to get dark outside and there was a chill in the air again, so Sarah lit a fire and closed the curtains. The glass was misted with the heat from the fire and the cold outside, but her eyes fixed onto something in the darkness. A shudder travelled through her and her whole body tensed as she turned to look at Jonathon who was still seated at the table. Then, turning to look towards the kitchen, she felt something grip her hand, preventing her from closing the curtain. Snatching her hand back, she squinted her eyes to look out through the misted glass. There was something, or someone, moving in the darkness outside. Leaning closer to the window, a cold shiver filled ran through her as her hands gripped the back of the chair tightly, her knees weakening beneath her. Her eyes widened and with a shake in her , she let out a screech, turning to Jonathon once again, this time with a look of terror on her face. Visibly shaken and with a trembling voice she said, "Someone's out there!"

"Who is? Who is it?" he said, getting up and running to the window.

"It's the figure from your painting, at the bottom of the garden. Looking straight at me and gesturing for me to go out."

Jonathon grabbed the poker from beside the fire and ran outside. "Who's there? Who's out here?"

As he did, Sarah grabbed hold of the curtain and pulled it closed with a quick sweeping movement to make sure her hand wasn't on it for too long. Jonathon ran down the road looking behind parked cars, and in every nook and cranny, but nobody was there.

Sarah turned to the painting and the figure had gone. Disappeared. The air in the room felt heavy and she struggled to breathe; it was as if she was drowning, gasping for every breath.

As Jonathon walked back in, Sarah grabbed hold of him. "Look at the painting. It's gone."

He looked at it. "What has, what's gone?"

"The figure, it's gone from the painting."

"Sarah," he said, gently, "it's there, I'm looking straight at it?"

She edged her way to the painting, "It wasn't there, I swear, it had gone. I couldn't breathe, I was suffocating, I felt like I was drowning."

Jonathon put his arm across her shoulders and pulled her towards him. "Are you sure you're okay. You should probably get some sleep. I'll check everywhere's locked up and let myself out, then put the key through the letterbox," he said. "I'll call you in the morning."

Agreeing it was for the best, Sarah cautiously made her way up the stairs, still shaking from the ordeal, her senses working overtime to try and make some sense of what had just happened.

CHAPTER NINE:

Jonathon arrived at Sarah's house early the following day and he checked all around the outside for any signs of foul play before she awoke. He knocked on the door and waited, but there was no answer, so he knocked again, only a little bit harder this time. He looked up to the window.

"Sarah!" he shouted, before he noticed her coming down the stairs through the glass in the door. "Sarah, are you okay?"

She stood at the other side of the door. "Leave me alone, there's something wrong with that bloody picture of yours. I want it out of my house, now!"

"Will you let me in," he said. "We can talk about it and if you want it gone, then I'll take it back to the gallery for you."

Reluctantly, she opened the door and let him in, leading him to the kitchen table where she made them both coffee. Sarah gripped the cup with both hands and stopped between sips to look up at the painting. "The figure wasn't there; I swear, I saw it in the front garden, and it wasn't on the painting. How do you explain that?"

"Nowhere people."

She looked at it, a questioning look in her eyes. "What do you mean, nowhere people?"

"I told you at the gallery. When I paint, I see them, they're in all of my paintings. I believe they're there for a reason; I just don't know what it is."

"To scare the bloody living daylights out of me?"

Jonathon walked over to the painting and stared at it. "Why did you buy it, what made you go back into the gallery and buy it?"

Sarah sighed. "This is going to sound silly, but when I went back to it, it kind of drew me in. I felt like I was a part of the picture. I was standing at the bridge looking into the forest, and all my senses were doubled, or tripled. I didn't just *feel* like I was in the forest, I think I actually *was* in the forest. My shoes were wet when I came back, and I thought it may have been from before I entered the gallery, but now I'm sure it was from walking through the forest. I tried to see the face of the figure; it was calling me towards it, but I couldn't get close enough to see. It was amazing and frightening, but at the same time fascinating."

Jonathon nodded slowly. "So, the very reason you bought it is the same reason you want to get rid of it, because you think 'The Nowhere Man' is trying to communicate with you."

"I'm frightened, Jonathon, can't you see that? That bloody painting will be the death of me."

Jonathon sat down on the sofa directly opposite the painting, and stared at it. He didn't even blink. "Who is 'The Nowhere Man' and why has he chosen you? Maybe, he's trying to tell you something."

Sarah sat with her back to it, a blanket wrapped tightly around her shoulders, and she was rocking back and forth in the chair. "I want to send the painting away, it's cursed," she said, clearly unable to look at it. "Anton told me it was cursed before I bought it. Whoever had it before me had sent it back."

"I don't think he'll give you the same money back that you paid for it."

Sarah looked him in the eye and said, "He doesn't want it back, it's cursed, burn it, I don't care about the money."

Jonathon had to concede; he could see how upset she was. "I'll pick it up later and take it back to the gallery," he sighed.

Sarah shook her head. "No, burn it," she said, abruptly.

"Okay, if that's what you truly want, I'll do it. I'll pick it up later today," he said, sighing again, then left the house, gently closing the door behind him. Sarah, meanwhile, felt alone and somewhat vulnerable, knowing the painting was still there and would be for a good few hours, yet.

After he'd gone, she went upstairs and stepped into the shower; the feel of the hot water running down her body seemed to take the stress away instantly. Placing her head under the flow of water, the pressure felt like a massage on the back of her neck. Cupping her hands and letting them fill with water she splashed her face, then took the shampoo and massaged it into her hair. The room began to fill with steam from the heat of the water and the glass of the shower cubicle became opaque. Sarah stood there for a few minutes, eyes closed, the water washing the suds from her hair and cascading over her soft white skin. Then, opening her eyes, she caught a glimpse of movement in her peripheral vision.

She froze, her eyes now wide open, her breathing heavy and her body trembling. "Jonathon, is that you?" she called out. Using her hand, she made a small circle in the steam on the glass, just big enough to see out towards the door.

Once her eyes adjusted to the steam in the room, she could see the shape in the doorway. The muscles in her shoulder tensed and she felt pain in her neck as her hands clamped onto the shower door. Absolutely every sinew of her body wanted to scream, but she couldn't make a sound. The figure had no features, no eyes, no mouth, but Sarah could hear a quiet voice. *"Help me."*

She opened her mouth and tried to force a scream, but no matter how hard she tried she couldn't make a sound.

She heard it again, *"Help me, please."*

The room filled with the scent of the forest, she remembered it from when she entered the painting in the gallery, and she could hear the sounds of the birds and hear the wind. The water began to rise in the shower cubicle and she started pulling at the handle with all her might, but the door wouldn't budge as the water rose, passing her waist and rising quickly over her breasts and onto her shoulders. Fear gripping her to her soul, she used every ounce of strength, but to no avail.

Her eyes transfixed on the figure as it seemed to disappear into the steam and suddenly Sarah could hear herself screaming and the water began to lower in the cubicle. She fell to the floor and curled up, the hot water beating down on her naked body, and she lay there for what seemed like an age, crying.

Eventually composing herself, she sat up, angry now at the thought someone could be taunting her. "Help who?" she said. "Who are you?"

She rose to her feet, switched off the shower and tentatively opened the shower door. Reaching out for the towel, she experienced a coldness like she'd never felt before. It was biting, a cold that she'd never known, like being hit with icy needles all over her body. Pulling the towel tightly around her, she nervously edged her way out onto the landing and warily made a dash for her room.

After drying herself and putting on her clothes, she made her way to the living room and looked at the painting. The figure was there. *Was this the same figure from the night before?*

She leaned on the fireplace and put her face close up to the man in the painting. "Who are you and what do you want from me?" Her face was almost touching the painting now, for what seemed like an age as she kept asking herself and the person in the painting questions. "Why choose me? What am I looking for? What are you looking for?" Then she began to search the whole painting for any clue as to why they had chosen her, and what for?

While she was standing there Jonathon came back. He let himself in through the front door. "Hey, what are you doing?" he asked, after seeing Sarah staring intently at the painting.

She turned to him. "You painted this, where are the clues? Where's the reason? Who is 'The Nowhere Man'? You have to know."

Jonathon shook his head. "I don't know, I honestly don't know."

"This isn't a game, Jonathon; I need to know! What about your other paintings? Can you find out where they are and who bought them? Maybe they can shed some light on what's going on here."

He shrugged and stood next to her. "They were all sold by agents or galleries, I don't have details of who, or where they are. I've only come back to burn the painting like you asked me to."

Sarah bolted out of the room and into the kitchen. Returning a few minutes later with her iPad, a note pad, and a pen.

"I've changed my mind," she said. "We're not burning it. I want to know who that is." She pointed at the figure. "Has Anton sold any others for you?"

"No. This is the first one, but I know it was returned. We could ask why it was returned and who sent it back."

"Okay, you call Anton and see if you can get the details and then we sit down and find out who and where the other agents."

Realising there was no point objecting to Sarah's determination, Jonathon set himself up at the kitchen table while Sarah set up office in the lounge. He called Anton and asked him whether he could provide some details about the person who had previously bought the painting.

"I'm not sure I can give out those details," Anton said, reluctant to tell him.

"Look, Anton, I have a problem here. Sarah, the lady who bought it the other day has become obsessed by the figure in it and it's starting to cause her some stress. Couldn't you break confidentiality just this once and tell me?"

Anton hesitated for a few moments, then said, "I've actually sold the painting twice before and each time it was returned with a similar story. People having bad dreams, hearing voices and being aware of someone or something in the house, but none of them saw anything that I'm aware of."

"Can you please text or email me their details and I'll try to get in touch with them?"

"It's very unusual for me to give out that kind of information, but just this once…"

"Thanks, Anton," Jonathon said, standing up and going to the lounge where he sat opposite Sarah at the table.

"Anton's sending me the contact details for the people who've previously owned the painting and returned it," he said, hoping that might calm her.

"People? There was more than one?" she asked, not at all calm. Sarah remembered Anton saying he'd sold it before and had it returned because it was unlucky. "When he said unlucky, I thought he meant like the old paintings of the little girl crying. They were meant to be unlucky, but they never stood in your front garden or in the doorway of the bathroom. This isn't bad luck, it's more like a curse. It's just plain weird..."

Jonathon interrupted. "It was in your bathroom? Today?"

Sarah nodded. "Yes, frightened the freaking life out of me by trying to bloody drown me, and then asked me for help. I really need to find out what it wants from me." She opened Google and entered 'artist agents' into the search panel. "Let's start with area. What area did you sell the other four? Were they all sold locally? If we have a location, we can locate the agents and hopefully find the buyers."

"I can tell you the name of the first agent, he was based in Liverpool. His name was Kendall, Joseph Kendall."

"Should be easy enough to locate," Sarah said, tapping away frantically. "Here he is. He's in a studio near the docks."

She wrote his number on her pad and asked Jonathon whether he remembered any other names.

"Anthony Prescott. He was in York when I last spoke to him, but I'm sure he left the country a few years ago."

"I'll search for him, too, and in the meantime, you call Joseph Kendall."

CHAPTER **TEN**:

Jonathon went back to the kitchen starting dialing Joseph Kendall's number. Engaged. After a few attempts, he finally got through.

"Hello, is that Joseph Kendall?"

"Yes, it is, how can I help?"

"My name is Jonathon Ripley; I need your help to locate one of my paintings that you sold for me a while ago."

"Does the painting have a name, Mr Ripley?" Joseph asked.

"I called it 'Forbidden'. I really need to locate the person who bought it."

"I'm afraid I couldn't possibly divulge that information; it's confidential."

"Please, Mr Kendall. I really need to find the owner. Could I come to meet you to discuss this further?"

"You're more than welcome to discuss the painting with me, but I'm afraid I won't change my mind about giving out my customer's personal information."

Jonathon sighed. "I understand. Thank you for your time," he said, before ending the call.

"I've found an Anthony Prescott, formerly from York," Sarah said, after hearing Jonathon finish his call. "He's now based in Southern Spain. Looks like he made a few quid out of selling art."

"Joseph refused to give us the details, but he's willing to meet with us. He could have some information even if he won't give us the buyer's details."

"We'll go to see him tomorrow morning. Maybe a woman's gentle persuasion will help," Sarah smiled, before going back to her iPad and continuing her search for contact details on Anthony Prescott.

"I don't suppose you kept his number or any other details when you gave the painting to him?" she asked.

Jonathan pondered for a moment. "I've probably got a receipt somewhere at home, but I have no idea where it would be."

Sarah put her head in her hands and thought for a few minutes. "Did you have an accountant?"

"Yes, he's based in the village. I'm not sure he'd have kept copies for this long, though. I sold that painting in 1996."

"Worth a try. Give him a call and ask. We'll never know if you don't ask."

"Bossy, aren't you?" Jonathon said, as he began to scroll through his mobile to find his number. "Well, it's not under G, or S. I must have deleted it."

"Have you tried A for accountant?"

Jonathon smiled at Sarah as if to say, *Don't be stupid* before typing ACC into his phone. "Ahhh, there it is, good job you're here." He pressed the call button and waited. Within a few rings, the call was answered. "Geoffrey, it's Jonathon, Jonathon Ripley. You used to do my accounts a few years back, well, a lot of years back. 1992 to 1998 to be exact." He knew he was starting to ramble. "Anyway, I was just wondering how long you keep accounts for. I need a receipt for a painting, you see, that I sold back in 1996. Don't suppose you can help?"

Geoffrey was silent for a few seconds before he spoke. "Jonathon Ripley, the painter and book cover artist?"

"Yes, that's me, you have a great memory, I'm very impressed."

Geoffrey laughed. "My memory is good, but not that good. However, fortunately for you, my computer does have a very good memory, and your files were uploaded in 2000 and also, fortunately for you, I've never cleared old files. Call me an optimist, but I always hope that people will come back to me at some point."

"I'm so glad you're an optimist, there are far too many pessimists in this world," Jonathon said, smiling, noticing Sarah's impatient expression.

She tapped on the table. "Get to the point," she said.

"Geoffrey…"

"Call me Geoff by all means. Is it okay if I call you Jon?"

"Oh, er, yes, I suppose so. The thing is, Geoff, I'm looking for a copy of a receipt for a painting I sold to a man named Anthony Prescott in 1996. It was for a painting that I called, 'Dark Places'. Do you think you could find it in the files on your computer, or would receipts have been thrown away?"

"Once again, you're in luck. I had all receipts and hard copy paperwork scanned to a hard drive a few years ago. If you just give me a minute, I'll have it for you."

After a short silence and some clicking around on his computer, Geoff came back to the phone. "Twenty-eighth of July 1996. A receipt for one painting from A.L.P Art, signed by Mr A L Prescott. Would that be what you are looking for?"

"That sounds like it, Geoff. Would there be an address or any contact details on there? I'd very much like to contact Mr Prescott."

"There's an address and a landline number. Would you like those?"

"Yes, please, that would be much appreciated. Could you text them to this number?"

"I'll do it straight away," Geoffrey replied. "It was very nice speaking to you again, Jon. If you need my business in the future, do get in touch."

Jonathon hung up and gave Sarah the good news.

"How is that good news? We have an address he no longer lives at and a twenty-odd-year-old number for a house in York. Did you not hear me when I said he's moved to Southern Spain?"

He sat back in the chair. "Family! He might have left family in the house. They might even have the same number. It's a start, more than you found on bloody Google."

Sarah huffed. "I found the people who live there are called Johnson. That's not Prescott!"

Jonathon shook his head in disbelief. "Maybe, just maybe, Mr Prescott had a daughter, Miss Prescott, who married Mr Johnson and they are now the Johnsons."

Sarah gave a knowing grin and asked Jonathon to call the number.

"I'll call them as soon as I receive the text from Geoff," he said.

She checked through her notes. They now had two of the agents' details: Joseph Kendall, who sold the 'Forbidden' painting, and possibly Anthony Prescott who sold the painting entitled 'Dark Places'.

"Do you remember any other agents' names?"

"There was only one other agent. The last two I sold were sold through galleries, including the one that you bought." He thought for a moment. "She was based down near Crewe. I can't remember her name, but I'm almost certain that her company began with the letter B, and mainly sold online."

Sarah began scrolling through the agents based in, or around Crewe. "Braithwaite's? Could that be it?"

"No. That doesn't ring a bell."

"Banner and Charles?"

"Nope."

"What about Bradley's?"

"Now, that sounds familiar. Bradley… Bradley… Erm, Lindsay Bradley. That's it," he clicked his fingers and offered a huge smile. "Lindsay Bradley."

Sarah copied down the office number and passed it to Jonathon. "Before you call, can you remember the name of the other gallery?"

"Not a clue. It was on a high street in a village in Wales. They'd seen a picture I shared online and asked if they could buy it. It was a couple of years ago so I'm sure if I were to search through my social media, I could probably find it"

"Call Bradley's first and then we'll bring up your social media accounts."

"We? I can search my own accounts thank you."

Giving Sarah a sarcastic salute, Jonathon called Bradley's but the phone just rang out. He tried a few times, but eventually concluded that the office was probably closed. "Maybe they only work a few days a week. I'll try them again in the morning when we go to visit Joseph."

CHAPTER **ELEVEN**:

S arah scanned through her list again. "We have definite contacts for the first painting and the third, and I have the fifth. We also have a possible contact for the second painting, if Mrs Johnson, by some miracle, turns out to be related to Mr Prescott. The fourth painting was put into a gallery in North Wales." She looked at Jonathon. "We need to find that gallery in North Wales. Get onto your social media and start searching. If you can locate the gallery, we should have the full set."

He scrolled through his Facebook, searching through his media photographs. "There's hundreds of them. How am I supposed to find one? It's impossible."

"What was the name of the painting?"

"'Dream Catcher'."

"Put that into the search. It should find it if it was mentioned by you, or the buyer."

He did as she asked. "I've got it. It's in a small village near Abergele. The name of the gallery was Paentiadau a Phrintiau. I've even got the postcode."

"Excellent work, Jon. I'll check for a contact number and we've got a full set."

Jonathon raised his eyebrows "Jon? You called me Jon."

"Yes. You told your friend Geoff that Jon was fine, so I assumed if it were fine for Geoff, it would be fine for me?"

"I needed something from Geoffrey. How would you like me to call you Sare?"

"Call me what you want, just make sure you call the gallery first."

Shaking his head, he dialed the number for the gallery and the phone was answered almost immediately. "Bore da sut alli I."

"Sorry, I don't speak Welsh," Jonathon said, pulling a face at Sarah. "My name is Jonathon Ripley. You purchased one of my paintings a few years ago and I'm trying to trace it. Would you be able to help?"

There was a pause before the answer. "It would have to be a very distinctive painting for anyone to remember who it was sold to. We sell many paintings and very few are registered to a buyer. They are mostly purchased for hanging in homes."

"You contacted me through my Facebook page and asked if you could buy it," Jonathon said, hoping it would jog a memory. "I have a photograph of it on my phone. I could send it through if that'll help?"

"Do you have our email address? It would be better to email it."

"Yes, I do. It will be with you in a few minutes. Could you please call me back once you've had a chance to look at it?"

Sarah checked the time: 3.45pm. She strolled to the kitchen and called back to Jonathon to ask whether he would like a sandwich and a cuppa.

"We haven't eaten all day," he said, hitting 'send' on the email. "A sandwich would be lovely, thanks."

While she made the sandwiches, she shouted to Jonathon, "Do you think they'll call back today?"

"Well, I hope so, somebody there must remember the painting. It was one of my best. Although that's only my opinion and I'm slightly biased."

Just as she entered the room with the sandwiches, Jonathon's mobile started to ring.

"Hello, Jonathon Ripley speaking."

It was a woman's voice on the other end of the phone. "We tried to call you a number of times, Mr Ripley. We sold the painting to a young couple, but they returned it a couple of weeks later. They insisted that we took it back from them and weren't interested in us returning their money, although we did refund them. When we asked the reason for returning it, they said that it was causing upset in the home."

"Did they say what the upset was and how the painting could be causing it?"

"We didn't ask, they seemed very upset, though. I'd even go so far as saying that they were frightened by it."

"Do you know where the painting is now? Would you be able to contact the people who have it?" Jonathon asked.

"You're speaking to them. The painting is locked away in the cellar; you're welcome to collect it anytime you wish."

"How about tomorrow morning or perhaps Thursday, would that be okay?

"As soon as possible for me," she said.

"Just one last question," Jonathon added. "Do you have the details of the people who bought it?"

"We have the delivery address from the original purchase. I'm not sure whether they'd appreciate me passing their details on to you, but I can ask the question. I have a telephone number on the delivery note. I'll let you know what they say when you come in."

He put the phone down and turned to Sarah. She looked terrified. "What could possibly have made them return it? Were they seeing the same things as I have, or worse?"

Jonathon tried to calm her down. "It could simply be that they didn't like it once they'd put it up. We won't know until we can speak to them. Let's eat. We're both hungry. "

Sandwiches devoured, their next step was to decide on a plan of action for the following day. "Do we split up, seeing as the location of the galleries is quite far apart?" Jonathon asked.

Sarah fetched her map from the sideboard and laid it out on the table. Mulling it over, Jonathon said, "Liverpool is probably the best starting point to see Joseph Kendall, then Abergele, before heading down to Crewe. By then we should have the answers from Mrs Johnson also, so a trip over to York for the last leg."

"That looks like our plan then, Jonny boy," Sarah said with a grin.

"Jonny boy?! You're getting a bit adventurous with the names, aren't you? I prefer Jonathon. If you don't mind."

"Oh, lighten up, it's only a name. I bet you had worse than that when you were at school?"

"No. I attended a very strict school and nicknames weren't allowed. What was yours?"

"You'll laugh, especially after what's been going on here."

"Go on, I won't laugh. Honest."

"Sarah the Scarer! Great nickname for someone who's scared of her own shadow, eh?"

Jonathon did his absolute best not to laugh, but couldn't prevent a snort down his nose while trying to stop it. "I'm not laughing at you. I'm laughing at the thought of you being scared of your own shadow. You are definitely a lot stronger than most people. I would have been out of here like a shot if I thought I saw a figure in the garden, let alone in the bathroom."

"I didn't *think* I saw a figure," Sarah scoffed, "I actually *did* see one and believe me, I'm bloody terrified."

Jonathon stood up and picked up his coat. "It's getting late, I'd better head home. Early start tomorrow to get around these places and I'll have to empty my boot out to get the painting back from Wales."

"You're not seriously thinking of bringing that painting back here? Isn't one of these in this village enough?"

"I told them I'd collect it. It won't do any harm in the car. I'll put it somewhere safe when I get it back here."

He was about to leave when Sarah surprised him. "Would you mind staying," she said. "You can sleep in the spare room; I'll make it up for you. I really don't want to be on my own."

He pondered for a moment. "Okay, but I don't want you after my body later, I need my rest," he laughed.

"Believe me, no one is after your body. I'll just feel safer if there's somebody here."

She made up the spare bed and then went into her own room to change. After putting on her pyjamas and dressing gown, she headed back downstairs to join Jonathon.

"Is it okay if I have a shower?" he asked.

Sarah told him to make himself at home. "There are spare towels in your bedroom and a large white dressing gown in the wardrobe. It's much too big for me. My nan bought it for me years ago when she decided I was putting weight on."

They spent the rest of the evening in front of the fire, chatting about their upcoming trip. Then Sarah asked about his life and how he ended up in Stokley.

"I had a bit of a strict upbringing to be honest. Dad was a schoolteacher and Mum worked as a PA for one of the bosses at Woolworths. We lived in the Midlands until I was seventeen and then I moved up to Edinburgh to study art; well, that was the reason I gave to my parents. I could have studied closer to home, but I really needed some freedom. My ambition was to become a great landscape artist, and Cheshire is a beautiful part of the country, so, here I am."

"So, it was just the countryside that brought you to Stokley? No romantic tale of a beautiful maiden who stole your heart?"

Jonathon leaned back in his chair and shook his head. "No, unfortunately the only girl I loved was taken away to live in Germany by her parents."

"Why didn't you chase her?"

With a grin on his face, he replied, "Difficult to get flights when you're nine years old. She was the first girl I kissed, and we promised each other that we'd marry one day. It would be great to know what happened to her, not that she'd be interested in a failed artist, with horrendous debts, a gambling problem and no money."

Sarah's eyes widened. "Failed artist? Your work is fantastic, even if the figure in the painting I have *is* trying to scare me to death. Why haven't you ever looked for her?"

He shook his head. "I did, about seven years ago, but found out she's married with kids and she'd moved to Sweden with her rich husband." He shrugged. "Money wins again!"

"Maybe if you were to finish more paintings, stop gambling and pay off your debts, you could find yourself a soul mate?"

Jonathon lowered his head, let out a deep sigh, and replied, "That sounds lovely, and when you say it like that, it sounds easy. Believe me, I've tried. I honestly believe my day will come, I'll win the lottery, or a big inheritance will drop in my lap one day, and I won't need to worry about money. I can give up gambling, finish my paintings, and live the easy life. Until then, I'll stick with sketching and book cover design to keep afloat."

"Perhaps it's time we got some rest," Sarah said, realising he was getting a bit upset. Tomorrow was, after all, another day…

CHAPTER TWELVE:

In the early hours of that morning, Jonathon woke up feeling icy cold. He got out of bed and went to the radiator to turn it up, but it was hot, very hot. He checked the window, which was closed, no draught coming in.

Venturing out into the hall he found it was even colder. It felt like the depths of winter, but after checking the radiator in the hallway he couldn't understand why it was so cold. The radiator was on full.

He walked down the hall to where it changed direction towards Sarah's room and looked down the stairs to his left. The bottom of the stairs was eerily dark. He looked back towards his room and then turned to look along the darkened hallway towards Sarah's room. The door was slightly open with a glimmer of light, and he took a step along the hall, the floorboards creaking beneath his feet, making him stop and glance down before attempting to move again, worried he might wake Sarah. As he raised his head to look back at the doorway of Sarah's room, he could see a shadow to the side of the door.

"Sarah, is that you?"

As he spoke, the shadow turned and began to move along the wall towards him. He froze on the spot. "Holy shit, Sarah, are you okay?"

As the shadow approached, Jonathon cringed and closed his eyes, wrapping his arm across his face, his body set rigid, statuesque in anticipation of what horror the shadowy figure was about to bestow upon him. As it glided past him, he felt a shudder and an absolute bitter cold filled his body. He lowered his arm from his face as he turned to see the shadow disappear into the darkness at the bottom of the stairs and a clear orb seemed to linger for a few seconds before vanishing into the night.

"SARAH!" he said, his voice raised now. "Please answer me, are you okay?"

Sarah opened her bedroom door. "What's up?" she asked, sleepily.

"Didn't you see that thing. The shadowy figure and the orb. Didn't you see them?"

She stepped out of her room and walked towards Jonathon. "Was it the man from the painting? 'The Nowhere Man', was it him?"

Jonathon jstared at her, eyes wide open and with a quiver in his voice, said, "I don't know, I honestly don't know. Could it have been the lights from outside, or maybe the shadows from the trees? There has to be a logical explanation."

Sarah shrugged her shoulders and turned to go back to bed. "I told you, you wouldn't believe me, but I told you. He, or it, is real."

"Maybe I should sleep on the floor in your room, just in case it comes back."

"He won't come back now. It's getting light and the rooms feel too warm. Go back to bed, I'll see you in the morning."

Jonathon reluctantly went back to his room and sure enough, it was warm. He laid on his bed and tried to go back to sleep, listening out for the slightest noise. Unable to sleep, he took a chair and wedged it beneath the handle of the door, then put the other chair by the window where he intended to sit, having the outside and the door within his view. Dawn was fast approaching, but eventually he managed to fall asleep, albeit in an uncomfortable position.

He awoke to the sound of Sarah shouting him down for breakfast, and after rubbing his eyes and straightening up his dressing gown, he made his way downstairs.

"I think I had a terrible dream last night. Sorry for waking you up," he said, yawning his way towards the table. "There was a shadowy figure in the hallway, and the whole house was bitterly cold. Did you manage to get back to sleep okay?"

Sarah gave him a questioning glance and said, "What are you talking about. That was the best sleep I've had in a week. I don't think I moved from the second my head hit the pillow."

"No. You came out of your room and spoke to me. Either you're going insane or I am. You definitely spoke to me. You told me to go back to bed and the shadow wouldn't be back because it's nearly dawn."

"Well, I must have been sleep walking, or you *were* dreaming, because as far as I know I didn't move all night."

Jonathon started to eat his breakfast. He knew it wasn't a dream; it was too vivid. Or maybe it was a dream, and maybe the talk about the figure had caused him to have a nightmare. There was no chair against the back of the door this morning, even though he distinctly remembered putting it there. Whatever it was certainly scared the living daylights out of him.

Sarah went up to her room to get ready, choosing a dress that would be sure not to take away any of the attention from Jonathon. It was more important the agents they spoke to today took more notice of him than they did of her.

There first stop was Jonathon's house, where he got changed into smart trousers and a shirt, before they started their journey along the M56 towards Liverpool to meet Joseph Kendall. Sarah noticed he was being somewhat evasive and a little short with his answers whenever she asked him something.

"Have I upset you, Jonny boy?"

He stared straight ahead. "Actually, you have," he said, much to her surprise. "I've listened to all your stories about figures in the garden and figures in the house, all of which are blamed on my painting, and then I spent all day yesterday searching for owners of my previous paintings, and today I'm travelling around the North of England and Wales, all to help you out. But when it comes to me seeing shadows in the night, you completely dismiss it as a nightmare."

Ouch! "I apologise," Sarah offered, looking at him sheepishly. "I don't remember getting out of bed, so I just assumed it was a dream you'd had. Or a nightmare. If I'd remembered waking up and being in the hall, it would be a totally different conversation, but unfortunately, I don't." She was actually fully aware of what had gone on in the night, but was afraid that if she were to admit it, Jonathon would be frightened away. Right now, he was her only ally and she couldn't afford to lose him.

As they drove into Liverpool, Jonathon asked whether she had been there before. The impressive buildings along the waterfront were a sight to behold.

"I came a few years ago and did a tour of the city," she said. "The three buildings you see here are known locally as The Three Graces: The Liver Building, The Cunard Building, and the Port of Liverpool Building. They're the landmarks that you see when entering the city on the river. Liverpool is a very historical area, full of nautical history; we could have a day out here once we've sorted out the paintings."

They eventually arrived at Joseph Kendall's studio, a lovely looking old building, fitted with a new glass façade, which still maintained the old look but with a modern twist. Jonathon liked to think he knew a little bit about architecture, so he thought Sarah should learn a small bit about it and stopped her outside. "This is a typical eighteenth-century building, which has been perfectly…"

Sarah interrupted him in mid flow. "Really Jonathon, I'm not interested in the bricks and mortar. We're here to find out where your painting is. Which one was it that Joseph sold?"

Jonathon sighed at her petulance. "It's entitled, 'Forbidden'. It's a landscape painting of a beautiful meadow filled with yellow and white flowers and a wonderful, blue, summer sky."

"And a mysterious figure in the distance, obviously?" Sarah added.

"Yes. She was in the meadow amongst the flowers, too far away to recognise but close enough for me to put her in the painting."

There was a couple of people in front of them speaking to a man and pointing at the attractive-looking sculptures in the studio.

Sarah nudged Jonathon. "Is that Mr Kendall?"

"I'm not sure to be honest. I've ever met him once for a few minutes and it was quite a while back."

They strolled around the studio for a while, waiting for the man to finish his conversation, and whilst looking about, they came across an interesting sculpture. Sarah picked it up and began to rotate it slowly in her hands. "That's the figure, somebody has made a sculpture of the figure. It's not identical, but it's a very close resemblance."

Jonathon took a closer look and sure enough, it did look a lot like the nowhere people he included in his paintings. Unable to wait any longer, Sarah called across to the man and interrupted the conversation he was having with the couple.

"Excuse me, are you Joseph Kendall?"

He turned around on his heels. "Yes, I am. I will be finished with these clients shortly and I will come over to you then." Then he noticed her holding the sculpture. "Please be careful with that; you'll have to pay for it if you drop it," he said, turning back to the couple.

"Did you make this figure?" Sarah asked.

He sighed and looked at her again. "Yes. I am the culprit. If you give me a few minutes, I'll be available to help you."

"Did you copy this from a painting entitled 'Forbidden', by any chance?"

Joseph stopped just as he was about resume his conversation and immediately excused himself from the couple, making his way quickly over to Sarah.

"Sorry, I didn't catch your name."

"My name is Sarah; my friend here is Jonathon Ripley. He's the artist who painted 'Forbidden'."

He turned to Jonathon and held out his hand. "It's a pleasure to meet you, Mr Ripley," he said, as they shook hands.

Jonathon took the figure from Sarah and looked it up and down. "Why would you make a sculpture of a mysterious figure in a painting? It doesn't have a face or any personality, it's just a grey mass."

"It fascinated me from the first moment I set eyes on it," Joseph began. "I was drawn into your painting like never before. The vibrance of the colours, the incredible brush work, and the absolute beauty of the flowers in the meadow. I was taken in completely by it all, it made me feel like I could hear the birds singing, smell the freshly cut grass in the surrounding fields and hear the sound of the flowers blowing against each other in the breeze. It was amazing. So, I simply had to make the sculpture."

Sarah knew exactly what Joseph was talking about, having experienced the same feelings in the gallery when she first looked at the painting that she'd bought. Jonathon placed the sculpture back on the shelf.

"Do you know where the painting is now?" he asked.

Joseph's eyes lowered. "Sorry, I have no idea. I sold it to an elderly gentleman about eighteen months ago. He literally made me an offer I couldn't refuse."

"Do you have details of the gentleman, an address or a phone number? We really need to find the painting as soon as possible."

"I couldn't possibly give you his address, but I do know where you can find him," Joseph said. "He stops at the Style café on Water Street every morning around ten o'clock, for coffee and shortbread. His name is Jacob."

After thanking him, Sarah and Jonathon left the gallery and walked up to Water Street, which wasn't very far from Joseph's studio. It was half past nine, so they ordered a coffee and a bacon sandwich and waited. Sure enough, at ten o'clock, an elderly gentleman entered the café, took a seat by the window, and ordered a coffee and shortbread biscuit.

Jonathon walked over. "Sorry to disturb you, sir. Would you be Jacob by any chance?"

The man looked up. "Well, that would depend who was asking," he answered in a strong Irish accent.

"My name is Jonathon Ripley, you probably have no idea who I am, but I was told I might find you here and that you bought a painting, which I painted, from Joseph Kendall last year."

"You would be correct in your assumption; I *am* Jacob and I *did* buy the painting from Joseph."

"Would you mind if we joined you?" Jonathon asked. "We have some questions about the painting."

Jacob nodded. "Please do. You can ask me anything, but I'm not going to sell it."

Jonathon and Sarah looked at each other. "Why did you buy it?" Sarah asked. "Why do you want to keep it so much?"

Jacob settled back in his seat and said, "I often used to call in to Joseph's shop with my wife. Whenever we came into town, we would stop here at the Style café for a coffee and then we'd take a stroll along the waterfront stopping on our way to see the paintings and the sculptures in Joseph's studio. Last year I lost my wife to brain cancer. She was so beautiful; even at seventy-eight she lit up a room with her locks of grey hair and her wonderful smile. She was my life, my world and my everything. Losing her was like having my heart ripped from my chest." He stopped for a moment to wipe the tears from his cheeks and then continued. "A few months after she passed away, I thought I'd recreate our trip into town, hoping it would cheer me up. I called here, drank a coffee, then went for the stroll we used to take along the waterfront before calling into Joseph's studio." He paused again, before adding, "As soon as I entered, I saw the painting and was attracted to it. I stopped in front of it and was mesmerised by its clarity. I felt like it gripped me by the chest and pulled me in. The scent of the flowers was mesmerizing, the yellow and white of the petals were so vibrant against the brilliant greens of the stems. I could feel a gentle wind on my face, hear bees buzzing amongst the flowers and the sound of branches cracking beneath my feet. It was incredible. Then I saw the figure in the field. At first it was a grey blurred figure, but as I was drawn further into the painting, I could see her much clearer. As I approached her, she turned to look at me. It was my wife looking straight at me. There stood my beautiful Theresa, just like she looked the last time we walked through town together. I nestled down in the grass next to her and brushed the back of her hand. Her skin was so soft, like caressing rose petals. The painting restored my broken heart and I knew I just had to have it."

Sarah, dabbing tears from her own cheeks now, said, "That's probably the most wonderful thing I've ever heard."

Jacob smiled at her. "I have it hanging in the living room above my chair. Whenever I want to see Theresa, I look deep into the painting and there she is; even if it's only for a few moments, it makes my life worthwhile." He turned to Jonathon. "I owe you my life, sir. Thank you so very much for your work, it's magical and beautiful at the same time."

Sarah could have stayed and chatted to Jacob for the rest of the day, but after a few minutes, she and Jonathon stood up and bid him goodbye before they left the café, smiling from ear to ear.

"Well, Sarah," Jonathan started, "I wasn't expecting that. It definitely wasn't the horror stories we've been hearing, and you've been experiencing."

Sarah nodded. "No, it certainly wasn't. You created a new life for an old man."

CHAPTER **THIRTEEN**:

They got back into the car and sat for a few minutes, pondering what had just happened, before Jonathon started the engine.

"Let's get going," he said, "we need to get to Abergele as soon as we can if we're going to have any chance of getting to Crewe today."

The journey out of town was quiet and they were on Runcorn Bridge before Sarah broke the silence. "Jacob is truly reinvigorated by your painting. Who would have thought that a painting could spark such emotions in somebody? That was an eye-opener for me. Have you ever heard anyone speak so wholeheartedly about art?"

Jonathon nodded and smiled. "I grew up thinking that art can change a life. Many of the great painters say they can reach into your mind and your soul with a painting, a drawing, or a sculpture. I've always believed it, but never experienced it the way Jacob described it."

Settling back into her seat Sarah asked Jonathon why he'd stopped at five paintings. "What stopped you from doing more. Your paintings invoke such feelings and emotions that most people never get the chance to experience, whether they are good or bad feelings. For something you do to bring those out is a gift and you are wasting it."

"Money," he replied. "I stopped painting to concentrate on my sketching and book covers. They're much easier to sell and faster to turn around, and like I told you last night, I'm skint and have to earn a living."

"You have a talent, Jonathon; you need to embrace it. Finish your other paintings."

As they travelled along the A55 towards North Wales, Sarah tipped back her seat and fell asleep. Her mind drifting into a dream state, she found herself in the painting again, walking over the wooden bridge into the forest. The sounds were so clear, echoing through the mist. She could hear the most wonderful birdsong, like the music of Beethoven carrying on the droplets of fine rain, and the smell of damp wood of the forest. Ahead, in the distance was the figure; he seemed to be glancing over his shoulder and beckoning her to speed up, as if it was a game. She was walking faster and faster, until she broke into a jog, unable to feel her feet on the ground, as though she was walking on air.

He didn't seem to be moving very quickly, but as much as she tried, she couldn't catch up. Suddenly, somebody grabbed her by the arm and began to shake her. She could hear a voice. "Sarah… Sarah…"

Waking to the realisation that the voice was Jonathon's and the shaking was him trying to wake her up, she sat forward in her seat.

"We're here. Are you coming in?" he asked.

She looked through the car window at the front of the shop. It was a little, olde world shop set in between two charity shops and looked like it hadn't seen a lick of paint in years, the black pillars and name board faded by the years of sunlight and the gold coloured lettering flaking off. She walked over to the window and leaned forward to look in, but the window had a haze of dirt and grime, most probably from the exhaust fumes of the cars that had passed through the village over the years, and it was difficult to see in. Jonathon opened the door, which dragged on the old red lino. He looked down and there were black arcs gouged out of the flooring from the decades of use.

As they entered, Sarah was met at face height with taxidermy fox, standing on a wooden plaque. The fox looked horrified. She whispered to Jonathon, "They obviously didn't bother straightening its face after it had seen the gun."

She closed the door behind them and it hit a small brass bell on a spring-like mechanism hanging above it. "I wouldn't be surprised if Mr Benn doesn't come out. He'll have a closet at the back to take you to other places, dressed as a postman or a doctor." Just as she said it a man appeared from a doorway. "Here he is."

Jonathon stepped forward. "Jonathon Ripley. I called yesterday about the painting."

"Painting?"

"Yes, the painting you have in the cellar, the one that somebody brought back."

"Ah. Yes, you spoke with my wife. She'll be down in a moment; she's just having a bite to eat."

"We'll have a little browse around the shop while we're waiting, then," Jonathon said.

"We don't really call it a shop, it's a gallery. You'll find some really beautiful works of art in here and some really old prints showing the local area."

Sarah gestured with her head for Jonathon to go over to her. "Is it just me or is he really creepy?" she said in her best Welsh accent.

"Sssssh! We want this painting and the information about the people who bought it. Don't go and spoil it by winding him up."

"What's is this painting of anyway? I know it's called 'Dream Catcher' but what is it a painting of?"

"It's a landscape," Jonathon began, "looking through the valley of a mountain range with a forest of trees up each side. I stopped on the way up to Scotland to paint it. The nearest tree has a beautifully coloured dream catcher hanging from its branches, and in the distance amongst the trees is a man. It looks like he's lost in the forest, but he isn't. There's a town within walking distance, just beyond the trees."

"Can you see the town in the painting?"

"No, but I know it's there. It's where I was heading when I stopped to paint the valley."

The door behind the counter suddenly opened and a short, stout woman appeared, greying hair and a jolly face with rosy red cheeks.

"I believe you're here for the painting. Barry will go and get it for you while we discuss compensation."

Jonathon raised his eyebrows, glanced at Sarah, and asked the lady what she meant.

"Well, we couldn't sell it once it was returned, and the people who'd brought it back told locals that it was a terribly sad painting. I checked and we paid you seventy-five pounds for it, if I recall correctly. We only added a small margin when we sold it and we had to return the money when they brought it back."

Jonathon reached for his wallet while shaking his head. "Go on then, how much is it going to cost me?"

"A hundred and fifty pounds seems fair."

Jonathon reeled back in shock. "Hundred and fifty quid? I thought you said a small profit. That's a hundred per cent profit."

"No, Mr Ripley, I think you'll find it's fifty per cent."

Jonathon laughed. "Fifty per cent of seventy-five is thirty-two pound and fifty pence"

"Yes, Mr Ripley, but seventy-five pounds is fifty per cent of one hundred and fifty and that would be our profit."

Sarah burst out laughing. "She's only right Jonathon, she's only making fifty per cent on the deal."

Begrudgingly, Jonathon handed over the money and asked if she had the delivery note that she'd mentioned.

"I've spoken to them and they're happy for you to call, but they don't want the painting in the house."

"Could I have the address then, please?"

The woman rubbed her chin. "Well, it took a bit of time to get through to them, I probably lost some custom while I was upstairs calling them. And there's the cost of the call. Telephone calls are not cheap nowadays."

"How much?"

"A tenner should cover it."

Sarah opened the door and held it while Jonathon carried the painting out and placed it into the boot of the car.

"I don't think I've ever been done over so much by anyone before. She should be working for the Government. Imagine what she could do for the budget. She's just taken my rent money, so I hope she's happy," he grumbled as he started the engine.

They headed to the address sold to them by the not-so-jolly lady in the gallery and when they pulled up outside the house, there was a very smartly dressed young man in the doorway. As they walked up the pathway to the door, Jonathon held out his hand and asked, "Mr and Mrs Evans?"

"Gwyn and Linda. Please come in. Would you like a drink?"

"Two teas would be lovely, thanks."

Gwyn led them through to a small sitting room then scurried off to make the tea, returning a few minutes later with two steaming mugs. "Hope you don't mind mugs; we don't have cups."

Sarah gave him a smile. "Mugs are fine, I don't own any cups either."

"What made you take the painting back to the gallery?" Jonathon asked.

"Don't get me wrong, Mr Ripley, it's a lovely painting, but from the minute we brought it into the house weird things started to happen."

"Do you mind me asking what kind of weird things?"

"I hung it in the hall just to the right of the door as you come in and next thing I know, Linda is standing right up close to it, in some kind of trance. I had to drag her away from it."

Jonathon turned to Linda. "What was it that you were looking at?"

"It was like a magnet," she began, "I couldn't move away, and it was as if I was inside the painting. I could hear things so clearly. All my senses seemed to be heightened, the most beautiful blue sky and soft white clouds, the smells, the colours, the sounds all clearer than I'd ever experienced. I looked towards the dream catcher and I could hear the little bells tinkling, and the feathers hanging from it seemed to be dancing to the sound of the bells. I could even hear the pine needles dropping. Then I noticed a grey figure in the trees. I didn't move my lips, but I could feel myself shouting to him. He turned around and shouted something back to me, but I couldn't make it out. I tried to get closer, but I couldn't. He shouted again and again until I made out the name he was shouting. He shouted three or four times and I could hear it as clear as we're talking now." She paused for a minute and looked at Gwyn before continuing. "From then on it would drive me mad. Sleeping was impossible, and I could hear it all day echoing in my head. So much so, that we had to take it back."

"I understand," Jonathon reassured her. "I have the painting now and I'll either hide it away somewhere, or I might even burn it."

Linda lifted her head and her eyes widened. "No. If you do that, he'll never find her. The man in the painting, he's looking for someone and he seems to be lost. If you burn it, he'll never find her. Please don't burn him!"

Surprised at her outburst, Jonathon assured her he wouldn't burn it if that would ease her mind and thanked them both for their time, before he gestured to Sarah to get up.

"Come on, Sarah. We need to get to Crewe to see Bradley's."

As they began walking down the drive, Gwyn grabbed hold of Jonathon's arm as Sarah continued towards the car. "Is your lady-friend called Sarah?"

"Yes. Why?" he said, a puzzled expression now on his face.

"The man in the picture was shouting her name. That's the name that was driving Linda mad."

Jonathon patted Gwyn's shoulder. "I'm sure there are plenty of women called Sarah, but I'll let her know what you said."

CHAPTER **FOURTEEN**:

They hit the road to Crewe, and Jonathon tried again to call Bradley's. This time somebody answered.

"Bradley's. How can I help?"

"Hi, I'm trying to contact Lindsay Bradley about a painting she bought from me a few years ago. My name is Jonathon Ripley."

"I'm sorry but Lindsay is on leave, she won't be back for another few days. Is there anything I can help you with?"

Jonathon asked whether the gentleman had access to her books, and could he find out where or who a painting had been sold to. But he said that the only person with access to Lindsay's books was Lindsay herself.

"Do you have a number I can contact her on, or an email address that she would be checking while she's away?"

The man hesitated for a few moments. "I'll take down your number and if I hear from her, I'll ask if she's okay with me passing her number to you, or if she wants to contact you herself. What was your name again?"

"Jonathon Ripley."

Their last stop was going to be in York, but they needed to contact Mr and Mrs Johnson first, to check that they were related to Mr Prescott.

"Pull over into the next services, Jonny boy, we'll have some lunch and call Prescott's number."

Deciding to order a burger, Sarah excused herself and made her way to the ladies loos, while Jonathon found a table and contemplated whether or not to mention what Gwyn had said about the name. He was still mulling it over when Sarah returned and asked, "The story Gwyn and

Linda told us about what she'd seen in the painting, what do you make of it?"

"I think it ties in with the experience that you've had, and Jacob," he said. "You all had the feeling of being drawn into the paintings, you had the same enhanced senses, hearing things and seeing vibrant colours, and you've all seen something in the figures. The difference is that Jacob has had a joyous experience, whereas you and Linda were frightened by your experience. Although, feeling a little frightened, it was more about the repetitive..." He stopped himself before continuing with, "sounds in her head, rather than the painting itself."

At that point, the waitress came over and asked if they were ready to order. Jonathon reopened the menu and pointed to the burger and chips. "Two of those please, and could we have a pot of tea and a diet coke?"

"Well done?"

"Er... Thank you, but it really wasn't hard, I just pointed to the menu."

The waitress gave him a look of utter contempt. "Would you like your burgers well done?"

He rolled his eyes at Sarah. "Just one of my little jokes. Yes, please." The waitress wrote down their order then stalked off. "I hope she doesn't come back and say sorry about your wait. Because then I have to respond with: I know, it's because of all the burgers I eat. Another one of my little jokes, and she probably won't find that funny, either."

Sarah shook her head, smiled, and made the sound of wind blowing while gesturing with her hand like tumble weeds through the desert.

"Anyway. Going back to the paintings, one thing I have noticed is that the man in Gwyn and Linda's painting and the man in my painting seemed to frighten us, but the painting that Jacob had, with a female in it, was very loving and peaceful. Could it be that 'The Nowhere Men' themselves are the haunted ones, maybe they're characters in the mind of the painter, and his, or to be more exact, *your* mindset at the time of creating them has been transferred into the character of the figures?"

Jonathon flopped back in his seat. "Let me get this straight, what you're saying is, my mental state at the time of painting may have been transferred into my art. Correct?"

"Yes. Do you have anger issues with your father?"

"No, I don't. My father might have been strict, but he's a wonderful man. I've never so much as had an argument with him, let alone anger issues."

"What about male authority figures, teachers, or maybe policemen?"

"No, there isn't a male figure who I dislike enough to transfer it into my art. What a stupid suggestion!"

Sarah thought for a moment. "Before you call the number about the Prescott painting, tell me about it."

Jonathon pondered his answer before continuing. "Well; it's entitled 'Dark Places', which is nothing sinister, it was painted looking across a brook, which can be seen in the foreground, and on the other side is a woodland and thickets of trees. Within the trees there are dark areas, and at the time I remember thinking that they're like the parts of our minds that we rarely delve into. Areas that people with depression and anxiety visit during their lowest moments. Hence the name 'Dark Places'."

"Sounds wonderful, where is the figure in this one?"

"She's sitting in the woods, but she's quite faint because she's actually sitting in a darkened area."

Sarah leaned across the table. "I'll put money on it that this painting has made the owner happy."

Jonathon picked up his phone and dialed the number.

"It's ringing, at least it hasn't been cut off."

A lady answered. "Hello, you're through to the Johnson residence, Mrs Johnson speaking."

"Hello. My name is Jonathon Ripley. I was just wondering whether you may be the daughter or niece of Anthony Prescott?"

"No. I'm not. Is this a sales call? If it is then you're wasting your time, and mine. I have adequate insurance; my gas and electricity are taken care of, and the house is paid for."

Jonathon laughed. "I assure you this isn't a sales call; I sold a painting to a Mr Prescott back in 1996 and I'm trying to trace its whereabouts now. My problem being that Mr Prescott has moved away and I don't have any contact details for him."

"What did you say your name was again?" the lady asked

"Jonathon Ripley."

"Jonathon Ripley, Jonathon Ripley. It doesn't ring a bell."

"Do you know Mr Prescott?"

"He was my ex-husband. We ran the art company together, until he left in 2008."

"Do you have any records of the paintings you bought and sold?"

"I certainly do, I have photographs of every painting that went through the agency along with details of every owner."

Smiling, Jonathon asked whether he and Sarah could visit her and look through the photographs. "I'll recognise the painting as soon as I see it," he said, thinking she would be able to give him details of its new owner.

Mrs Johnson agreed to see them and gave them her address. Following her directions, through narrow country lanes lined with imposing, huge properties, Sarah strained her neck to see into some of the driveways as they passed them. "This is footballer territory, these houses must be worth millions," she said. "How the other half live, eh!"

Jonathon gave a forced grin and said, "Yeah. Maybe there *is* some money in the art business."

They eventually reached the gateway to the house and pulled up outside. Jonathon pressed the intercom and waited for a response.

"Enter when the gates are fully open. They're a bit slow so please wait."

The gates opened and the two of them sat in the car, eyes focused on the house in front of them. A beige gravel drive led through beautifully maintained gardens to a courtyard with a triple garage built from old reclaimed brick and large, dark oak doors with lovely old timber framed sash windows. The front door must have been ten feet high with gleaming black paint and shiny brass fixtures.

"This is amazing, Jonathon. That garage is bigger than my house and look at the views across the hills. This is a house of my dreams."

As they got out of the car, still admiring the property, they heard a voice shouting from around the side of the house, beckoning them to come around the back.

"Simply stunning," Sarah said in awe. "No other words can describe this; it's perfect. You should paint this!"

Mrs Johnson stepped out of the house and led them to a table and chairs in the garden.

"Would you like tea and cakes?" she asked.

Sarah looked at Jonathon and gave a little nod.

"Yes please, Mrs Johnson, that would be really good," he said.

"Please. Call me Emily, there's no heirs and graces here, we're down to earth Yorkshire folk."

When she disappeared inside the house, Sarah whispered, "If this is how down-to-earth Yorkshire folk live, then I was born in the wrong place."

Jonathan nodded. "I was thinking that myself. Seems like a lovely lady, though."

Emily came back with a tray carrying the tea and a folder, which she handed to Jonathon. She poured the tea and settled into a chair.

"Milk and sugar?"

"No, thank you, Jonathon said, then looked at Sarah. "Sarah, would you like milk and sugar? Emily is asking."

"Oh. Yes please, just one sugar. Sorry, I was engrossed in that view. It's wonderful and your home is so beautiful."

"Not bad for a girl from a little terraced house in Burnley. Took a lot of hard work to get here but it was all worth it, especially when you sit out here in the summer. Unfortunately, we take the views for granted now and really we should take time out to enjoy it more."

Sarah looked around. "I would sit here all day; nothing would ever get done."

Jonathon opened up the folder that Emily handed to him, and began to flick through the contents. He was very impressed by some of the art they'd handled. "Some of these paintings are worth a fortune, I'd be surprised if I find my piece in here amongst these."

Emily turned to him, and in a stern voice, told him that if anyone should know, then he should, that art is not about the worth of a painting to one man, it's about the worth to the person who sees the beauty within it.

"There are people who like Cubism, I personally wouldn't have it hanging in the toilet but that doesn't mean that I'm right. Art is all about opinion, it can be the tiniest thing within a painting that makes your heart beat faster and turns the whole painting into something of beauty."

This prompted Sarah to recall her conversation with Jacob in Liverpool earlier that day.

"We met a man earlier, who'd bought one of Jonathon's paintings because he was drawn into it by a figure he interpreted as his wife, who had sadly passed away. He paid the agent a lot more than it was worth because of that connection with the painting. So, I understand exactly what you're saying."

"I've always followed my heart," Emily began to explain, "when purchasing paintings over the years. The cost always far-outweighs the feeling that a painting or drawing gives me. I've never regretted buying or selling a painting throughout my whole career."

Jonathon suddenly looked up with a huge grin on his face. "That's it! That is my painting." He pointed to an image. "My art is in here with some of the greatest artists that have ever lived," he added.

"Show me which one it is, and I'll get the file for it," Emily offered. Jonathon rotated the photograph so she could see it. "J Ripley, the signature is J Ripley?" she asked. "If I'd have thought longer, I would have recognised it."

"You would have recognised my name out of all these fantastic painters? You'd have remembered me? That's amazing!"

Emily sighed, a look of despair clouding her attractive features. "I don't need to get the file; I know exactly where this painting is. It's in my ex-husband's home in Spain. He took it with him when he left and as much as I liked it, I'm sort of glad that he did."

"Why did he take Jonathon's painting over all of the others?" Sarah asked.

Emily let out another sigh. "I remember when we first got the painting, Anthony had recently lost a close friend and a family member in a car accident. He was in a deep depression and I was struggling to get him out of it. He spent hours on end sitting alone in the study and, no matter what I said or did, I couldn't get him to come out. I went to a small village in Cheshire to see a client and on that day, he was visiting an art's and craft's market in the town hall. That's where I saw the painting. I knew it would cheer Anthony up a bit as soon as I set eyes on it, so I bought it. I didn't even know the name of it at the time, I saw it written on the back a few years later."

"Was the village called Stokley by any chance?" Sarah asked.

Emily contemplated for a moment. "I think it was. Beautiful little village with a small grey-stone church."

Emily asked whether they'd like more tea before she continued with her story. They were both too interested in what she had to say so declined and asked her to carry on.

"I brought the painting home and took it into Anthony's study, placed it in front of him and he smiled, the first smile I'd seen on his face for a long time. He hung it in his study, and he would spend hours standing in front of it, just staring into it. Always with a slight smile on his face. I asked him what he saw when he looked into it and his answer had me in turmoil. On the one hand I was grateful that he was happy, but on the other hand it was taking him away from me."

"What was it that he saw?" Jonathon interrupted.

"He said that he didn't just look at the painting for hours, he felt like he was *inside* it. It was like a different world where the rippling of the brook was like music to his ears and he could feel the spray of the water on his face. The smell of the pines and the rustling sound of the trees was so beautiful. There was a beautiful lady, sitting in the shade of the trees in a dark place. He'd sit with her for hours on end, said her voice was so soft and so pure. When she smiled it would light up the dark places they were both in. His eyes would glisten, and he'd smile constantly while staring at it." Emily looked at the view for a moment, her eyes starting to glisten. "I'd lost him to a lady who, to me, was just a faint figure in a painting, but to him she was his light in the darkness."

Jonathon and Sarah sat in silence until Sarah said, "You lost your husband to a lady in a painting and yet you don't hate the painting or the artist?"

"As I said earlier, the beauty in art is in the eyes of the beholder. I would have lost Anthony to his depression or we would have drifted apart because we just didn't speak, the marriage was virtually non-existent. Don't get me wrong, we had many fantastic years together, he just never came back from the dark places in his mind."

Sarah sat back in her seat and asked Emily whether the cup of tea was still on offer. "I need one after that story," she said. "It was such a sad story, but with a kind of bittersweet ending."

Emily stood up. "I'll bring more tea and we can have a chat about your other paintings when I come back if that's okay with you, Jonathon. I'm assuming from how good 'Dark Places' was that you've done a lot more."

Emily returned with the tea, carrying a photograph under her arm, which she handed to Jonathon.

"This is the last photograph I have of Anthony before he left for Spain."

Jonathon looked at the well-dressed man, wearing a tweed jacket, tall and slim with thinning grey hair brushed back tight to his head, a grey handlebar moustache and pointed grey beard. He was leaning with his elbow on a against dark wood fireplace in what could only be described as a Victorian style room, with dark wooden panelling and a large bookshelf, filled with books. Above the fireplace was Jonathon's painting.

He handed the photograph back to Emily. "That's an excellent photo. He looks happy in it."

"He was. He's beside his treasured painting, which always made him happy."

Emily asked Jonathon about any other paintings he had and said that she'd like to look at them. "You never know, I might be in the market for another," she added.

Sarah jumped in. "He's only ever done five. I don't understand why someone with his talent stopped after just five."

Emily looked a little shocked. "You need to show your talent to the world, Jonathon. Such a terrible waste."

"I do have other paintings, but they're unfinished," Jonathon said. "Unfortunately, I didn't have the funds to continue and so turned to sketching and book cover work to earn a regular income."

"You have a real talent," Emily said. "Maybe you should complete those unfinished masterpieces and get them out onto the market. I would gladly look at marketing them for you."

With something to consider, along with their newly discovered information, they finished their tea and thanked Emily for allowing them to visit before heading back to the car.

"What did I tell you?" Sarah began, putting her seatbelt on. "The lady in the painting made him happy. That's a fifty-fifty split. Two men making people unhappy and frightened, and two women making people happy."

Jonathon put the key in the ignition and turned the engine over. "Well," he said, "that depends on your point of view, as to whether you class getting a divorce and losing your husband as a happy moment I suppose. I thought that was a very sad story really."

Sarah nodded. "It was sad that they divorced, but the female figure in your painting helped to bring a man back from the brink. That's definitely a happy ending."

As he put the car in reverse and began to press the acerlator, Emily appeared at the front door, waving at them. Sarah wound down her window.

"Just a reminder to allow the gates to fully open before driving through, and think about what I said regarding Jonathon's paintings."

It was late evening by the time they arrived back at Sarah's house, and Sarah was reluctant to go inside due to it being in darkness.

"Will you come in, just until I get the lights on and the fire lit?"

Jonathon smiled. "If you want me to," he said. Then added, "I'll nip home and get my overnight bag if you'd like me to stay over again?"

"I'd feel better if I came with you; I really don't want to go in the house on my own," she said.

"Then let's go back to mine and I'll pack a bag." He put the car in gear and added, "But there'll be no talk of shadows and ghosts tonight; I could do without another nightmare like the one I had last night!"

It didn't take long for Jonathon to get a few things together and he soon returned to the car and once more drove Sarah back home.

They got out of the car and walked up the path to the front door. But as they reached it, Jonathon stared in through the front window.

"There's somebody in there!" he said.

Sarah looked in, too. "Where?"

"Right in front of the fireplace, looking at the painting."

Sarah looked again. "I can't see anyone."

She opened the door and checked the living room, while Jonathon crept in after her looking around, wide-eyed.

"See? Nothing there. You're getting more paranoid than me," she said, switching the main light on.

Jonathon felt a bit better once the room was lit up and the fire began to roar, and settled himself down in an armchair while Sarah put the kettle on.

"Do you fancy a warm drink, or would you prefer a glass of something? I've got red or white wine, an unopened bottle of port, or there's some gin and a couple of bottles of tonic. What's your poison?"

"Let's have a couple of G&Ts, that should help with the sleep," Jonathon replied. "Have you got any ice?"

"G&T with ice and lemon, how does that sound?"

"Perfect!" he said, making himself comfy in the chair.

Sarah made their drinks then ran upstairs and quickly changed into pyjamas, dressing gown and fluffy slippers, before she headed back to the living room where she cosied up on the couch with her feet up bedside her. They polished off a couple of drinks and then Jonathon sloped off upstairs, bag in hand, to have a quick shower and get changed into his pyjamas, too.

"Let's just have another one, or maybe two before bed," he said when he returned to the living room. "A good gin and tonic never did anybody any harm."

Sarah, beginning to feel a chill in the air, nodded, then stood up and went towards the fireplace where she positioned herself with her back to the flames when suddenly, she felt the urge to turn and look at the painting. Once again, she found herself being drawn in, only this time she was already over the bridge and found herself in a clearing in the woods. The figure was just on the edge of the clearing, looking directly at her. She looked back and this time could see some shape to a face. It was too blurred to make out properly, but it was a lot clearer than the last times. From somewhere else, she could hear somebody shouting, as though in the distance: *"Sarah."*

She listened more intently and there it was again: *"Sarah."*

Then, realising she was back in the room, she heard it again. *"Sarah, Sarah."*

She looked at Jonathon, who was starting to nod off in the chair. Giving him a nudge with her foot, she whispered, "Jonathon, can you hear that voice? It sounds like it's coming from outside."

He shook his head. "What's it saying?" he asked.

"It sounds like somebody calling my name over and over, but it's from out there in the street."

He suddenly remembered that the painting they'd picked up was still in the back of his car. Should he tell her what Gwyn had said, or just hope the voice would stop?

"You sit down, I'll go and check whether anyone is out there," he said, reluctantly standing up. He grabbed his keys on his way out and ran straight to his car, then he opened the boot and gave the painting a shake, not knowing whether it would make any difference or whether Sarah was still hearing the voice. Then he headed back in.

"Nobody out there. Has the voice stopped?" he asked.

"Yes. It stopped while you were outside. I think I might have had a few too many gins." Sarah shrugged and rolled her eyes. "I'd better get to bed."

Jonathon smiled. "Okay," he said, "goodnight, Sarah."

She leaned over and gave him a peck on his cheek, lingering for a few seconds to smell his aftershave. "New day tomorrow, Jonny boy. Maybe Bradley's will call, and we can complete the set."

CHAPTER **FIFTEEN**:

After a quiet and undisturbed night, Sarah woke up and headed downstairs to make breakfast. Opening the curtains, she noticed that Jonathon's car had gone. She stood at the foot of the stairs and called out his name, but there was no answer. Reaching for her mobile phone off the coffee table, she dialed his number, and much to her surprise, he picked up.

"Where are you?" she asked. "I was just about to make breakfast."

"Just on my way back, I had to call at home for something."

"I was going to make us some breakfast; are you coming back?"

"Yes," he said, "I'll be there in ten minutes."

Just as she was putting their eggs on a plate, Jonathon arrived back at Sarah's house, beaming from ear to ear.

"I've received an email from the man we spoke to at Bradley's," he said, excitement in his tone. "He's sent me Lindsay's number but asked that I don't call her until after two o'clock."

"That's good news," Sarah said, carrying the plates through to the dining room. "You can tell me about the last painting over breakfast."

"It's probably one of my best," Jonathon began, picking up his knife and fork. "It's a lake with a beautiful little house on the banks. I painted it from the far side of the lake. The water was like glass, no movement at all, and in the background is a lovely woodland that blends into the distant snow-capped mountains. There's an empty boat sitting on the lake and the house has a little garden, filled with flowers."

"Where is the figure in this one?" Sarah asked through a mouthful of food.

"He's standing on the bank of the lake to the side of the house with his reflection in the water."

"He? Going by previous events, that means trouble."

"You're jumping to conclusions," Jonathon said, laughing. "Let's just see what she says later."

They spent the next few hours in the garden, and Jonathon proved his worth as he helped Sarah with the weeding and helpfully mowed the lawn. It was getting close to two o'clock when he approached Sarah, her hands filled with weeds and soil, a few smears on her cheeks.

"What time is it?" she asked.

"It's ten to two. Do you think I should leave it for ten minutes, or call her now?"

Sarah put the weeds in the bin bag next to her. "Leave it until two, she may be in a meeting," she said, rubbing the soil off her hands. "Two o'clock seems a fairly accurate time so ten minutes isn't going to matter too much to us."

As soon as the clock hit two, Jonathon pressed the button on his phone to make the call.

"Hi, you're through to the voicemail of Lindsay Bradley, please leave a message after the tone and I will call you back as soon as possible."

Jonathon tutted, disappointed that he hadn't got to speak to Lindsay herself, then left a short message explaining why he'd like to speak to her and finished the call by leaving his number.

"I'll give it half an hour and then try again," he said. "In the meantime, she might ring back."

They both sat at the patio table for a few minutes in silence, and then, much to their surprise, his phone started to ring. He looked at the screen. "It's her," he said, excitedly, before hitting the answer button. "Hello, Mrs Bradley?"

"Miss Bradley," she corrected him. "Is this Jonathon? I've just listened to your message. Which painting are you looking for?"

"It was a painting entitled 'The Lakehouse', signed J Ripley, and it was a painting of a lake, a treescape, and snow-capped mountains."

"I recall it well," she said. "It was sold three times and each time it was returned after a few days; I think the longest somebody kept it was two weeks."

Jonathon looked at Sarah, questioningly. "Why did they return it?"

"Well," Lindsay said, "each time it was returned the customers gave me the same story. They all heard voices, apparently. Personally, Mr Ripley, I'm very sceptical when it comes to that sort of thing, but after three times, I eventually gave up."

"Do you have any idea where it is now?"

"Yes. It's in my garage under the work bench, wrapped in a sheet. You're welcome to collect it, but the last person vandalised it by scratching their name into the side on the boat. Terrible waste because the painting was excellent."

"Do you remember the names of the people who bought it? I'd very much like to speak to them," Jonathon asked.

"I can check through my records when I return to the hotel to see whether I still have them."

Jonathon nodded and smiled, making a thumbs-up sign to Sarah. "That would be great, thank you. Would you be able to email them to me, please, and I'll contact them? When would be a good time to collect the painting? I may be able to repair the damage for you."

"I'm home late tomorrow night, so you could collect it on Thursday, any time after ten. And I really don't want it back, thank you all the same."

"Thank you very much for your time, Miss Bradley, and I look forward to receiving the buyer's details." Then, just before he ended the call, he added, "Enjoy the rest of your holiday."

"Well? What did she say?" Sarah asked, sitting up straight in her chair.

"Sorry, I thought you could hear. She said the painting is in her garage and I could pick it up on Thursday."

"Did she say why she still had it?"

"She said it had been returned by the previous owner. Well, she actually said owners, as in plural."

"How many owners had returned it and what were their reasons? Did she tell you that?"

He leaned back in his chair. "Well, the first two returned it because they could hear voices and the last one returned the painting after vandalising it, so she said. I told her I'd collect it and try to repair the damage."

Sarah went into a tirade of abuse, asking why he would even think about collecting another painting, which was obviously unlucky, or cursed. Especially when he knew that the one she had was causing her to have nightmares and see figures in the night, that the one Gwyn and Linda had was driving her insane and had been locked away in a cellar, and the one he was thinking of collecting had been returned three times!

"What's possessing you to want to bring another of those frightful paintings back. Are you trying to drive me insane?"

"Sarah, you need to take a little step back and think about this. We need to know what's going on. Lindsay is sending me the contacts for the people who bought it, so we'll go and see them, and, if the stories are too bad, or if you think you can't handle seeing the last painting, we can leave it where it is."

Sarah folded her arms and lowered her head.

"When is she sending the names?"

"When she returns to her hotel, so hopefully this afternoon."

"Did she say where the buyers live or if they're in the UK?"

"No, she didn't, but we can only try." He stoop up and picked up his phone. "Look, I need to go home and get on with a few things, but I'll be back soon. I'll keep checking my emails in case she sends the information through."

Sarah reluctantly agreed and watched him walk to his car then drive away. Deciding to while the time away, she went back to the weeding, and finished straightening up the borders before heading into the house to take a shower. She wanted to shower before it started to go dark, especially after the last time.

Following a peaceful shower, this time without any interruptions from scary figures or shadows, she put on her dressing gown and lay down on her bed. Within minutes she'd fallen asleep, until she was awakened by the creaking of a door downstairs. It sounded like there was someone in the house.

Dawning on her that she hadn't locked the back door, she crept out of bed and picked up the nearest thing to hand, an old brass candle holder, then edged her way out into the hallway and along to the top of the stairs, expertly avoiding the creaking floorboards, which was a feat in itself due to the fact she was shaking with fear. *Is there an intruder in my home?*

She made her way slowly to the top of the stairs and strained to see over the bannister. Creeping down, trying not to make a sound, her weapon above her head and ready to strike, she eventually reached far enough that she could see into the living and dining rooms. They both appeared empty, unless, of course, the burglar was hiding behind the couch.

Backing up towards the wall at the side of the kitchen door, she noticed a light in the kitchen. It wasn't a bright light. *A torch?*

Sarah took a deep breath and pushed the door open a little. The only light was coming from the fridge, its door slightly ajar. Maybe she'd left it open earlier, but then she noticed that the back door was slightly open, too. She edged towards the back door and slammed it shut.

There was an almighty scream and a figure jumped up outside the door.

Sarah reeled back and let out a scream of her own.

"GO AWAY! I'll call the police! You're trespassing."

"It's me, you silly woman." Jonathon stood there, seemingly alarmed at the candle holder she still brandished above her head. "What are you doing creeping up behind me like that? You scared the bloody life out of me!"

Sarah lowered her arm and scoffed. "I scared you? What the hell are you doing creeping around my house while I'm asleep? I thought you were a bloody burglar."

"I got the email off Lindsay, and I rushed back to tell you and the front of the house was in darkness, so I came around the back and saw the back door open. I didn't come in. I just sat by the door in case someone tried to break in. Anyone passing could have seen it and just walked in, so I pulled it shut and waited."

"Why didn't you sit inside?"

"I didn't want to frighten you, ironically."

Sarah closed the back door and locked it, then closed the fridge door, too. "I'll put the kettle on," she said, putting the candle stick on the worktop, much to Jonathon's relief.

Once they'd both calmed down, they started to laugh and Jonathon pointed to the candle holder. "You couldn't knock the skin of a rice pudding with that. What was your plan? Tickle them to death?"

They were still laughing when they moved into the living room. Sarah settled into her usual spot on the couch and Jonathon sat himself down in the armchair by the window.

"That was probably the funniest thing I've seen in years. Your face was a picture," she said.

Composing himself, Jonathon said, "Anyway, getting back to the reason I came over. Lindsay sent me the details of the buyers, and they're not too far apart. First one is in Newcastle-Under-Lyme, second one is in Malpas, and the last one is near Winsford. So, we could do them in that order and Winsford would be on our way back."

"Okay," Sarah said, nodding. "Do you want me to pick you up, or are you coming for me?"

"I'll have to call them in the morning, so I'll pick you up at half-past nine. Will you be alright on your own tonight?"

Sarah looked around the room. "I doubt anything in the painting could scare me more than you just did," she said with a snigger.

"Make sure you lock the door after me," he said, grabbing his coat. I'll see you tomorrow."

"I'll be checking all the locks as soon as you've gone, don't worry," she said, smiling at the thought he obviously cared so much.

Once she'd been through the house, checking doors and windows, she made herself a coffee and headed through to the living room, carrying a few logs under her arm to make a fire. Kneeling in front of it, she placed some newspaper and kindling at the bottom, lit a fire lighter, and pushed it in, and after a few minutes it was burning nicely, so she added the logs and sat herself down, looking into the flames.

The wood hissed and crackled as she watched the flames dance in the hearth, but then, she tensed as one of the hissing sounds became louder than the others and seemed to be lasting longer. She thought the noise it made sounded familiar, like someone whispering her name: *"Sarah."*

Using the poker to move the logs about, she heard it again, hissing in a kind of whisper, *"Sarah."*

Feeling alarmed now, she stood up and her eyes became fixed onto the painting in front of her. Once again, she was drawn in, and as with the previous time, she was beyond the bridge, in the same clearing. The figure standing across the clearing was looking directly at her, its face containing more features than the previous time, but she wasn't close enough to make it out properly.

For the first time, she spoke to the figure. "Come closer. I want to see your face."

The figure stood still, but it slowly nodded its head. She could just about hear a word, whispered, as though in the distance: *"Soon."*

She tried to walk towards it but she couldn't move forward. It didn't matter how hard she tried; it was an impossible task.

She turned around then and was out of the painting again, standing in the living room of her house. The figure wasn't frightening this time; it was calm and seemed to want to speak with her. Making herself comfortable on the couch once more, she continued to watch the flames, this time with a feeling of calmness as if a weight had been lifted from her shoulders. She was now quite sure, for the first time, that she wasn't in danger from 'The Nowhere Man' in the painting, after all.

CHAPTER **SIXTEEN**:

As the dawn chorus of the birds began, Sarah awoke, refreshed from a good night's sleep. The distant roar of a tractor engine could be heard in one of the fields and she sat up in bed, stretching and yawning. *This is going to be a good day. I can feel it in my bones.*

Getting out of bed, she slid her feet into her slippers opened the curtains, and looked out across the fields, littered with vibrant yellow flowers. She loved the sight of rape seed, its brilliant yellow as far as the eye could see. The sun was just rising, and the sky was lit up with its early morning colours, reflecting off the clouds.

It was too early to call Jonathon, so she made her breakfast of two freshly cut doorstep toast with plenty of butter and strawberry jam, then poured herself a cup of tea and went into the garden.

At nine-thirty on the dot Jonathon pulled up outside the house, beeping his horn.

"You look happy. How did you sleep?" he said, watching Sarah skip towards the car.

"I had the best sleep ever. I think I made peace with the figure last night and it's really lifted a burden," she answered, opening the car door and climbing in.

"Oh? How did you make peace with a painting? What happened?"

"I found myself drawn into it again, but this time I was facing the figure in a clearing. I could make out some features of the face, which made it less frightening, though I couldn't get close enough to see properly. But I spoke to it, asking it to come closer. It couldn't and I couldn't move towards it, but I heard a whisper."

"What did it say?"

"Just one word: *'soon'*. That was it."

Jonathon gave a little shrug of his shoulders as Sarah fastened her seatbelt.

"Well, I managed to speak to the first people on the list, William and Jane Owens in Newcastle-Under-Lyme. I got through to the second number and he said he'd speak to his wife before agreeing to meet us. I did try the third person but there was no answer, so I'll try again later."

"What did you say to the Owens to get them to allow us to call?"

"Just told them that I was the artist and I'd be interested in finding out why they returned the painting, and they agreed to see us." He put the car in gear and started to drive, both of them looking forward to what the day might hold in store.

It was less than an hour to the Owens' home, which was in a lovely little town dotted with thatched cottages amongst some newer houses, probably built in the 70s or 80s, Sarah imagined, though their mock Tudor facades tried to give them more character.

Jonathon pulled up at the side of the house, and they walked around to the front. As they opened the gate, Sarah saw a girl in the window and gave her a little wave. The girl quickly turned her head away as if a bit shy. They rang the doorbell and the door was opened within seconds by a lady who looked to be Turkish or Greek. She nodded her head in greeting and then a man popped his head around the door from a room at the end of the hall.

"Come in, please, we're in the back room," he said with a friendly smile. "Come in, sit down. We don't have a lot of visitors, so the place isn't really set out for them."

They followed the man into a poky room with only one small chair, a two-seater settee and a couple of chairs at a table, which was littered with books.

"Please, find a seat anywhere. Jane is in the front room with our daughter, Elizabeth, and our maid, Zeynep, the lady who opened the door to you."

He shouted Jane to come through and then asked if they'd like a cup of tea or coffee.

"Tea would be lovely, thank you," Sarah responded.

He disappeared for a few moments then came back, a petite-looking woman scurrying behind him, sunken eyes and grey-thinning hair. She sat on one of the chairs by the table.

"This is my wife, Jane," he said, and the woman smiled. "Zeynep will bring us some tea in shortly."

Sarah looked at Jane and felt sad for her. "Good morning, Jane, it's good of you to allow us into your lovely home," she said. Jane just gestured with a slight nod and a movement of her eyes.

Jonathon shuffled on his seat as Zeynep came in with a tray of cups and saucers, and a plate of biscuits. "Thank you for seeing us. The painting I'm interested in is of a lake house; it's actually one of my favourites. Would you mind telling me how you came to buy it from Lindsay?"

"We've purchased quite a lot from Bradley's over the years," William began, "they sell books and antiques as well as art. We called in looking for books to add to our collection and the painting was in the window. Jane fell in love with it and said it would be lovely above our fireplace. So, I bought it."

"Bradley's delivered it the next morning and Bill put it up as soon as it arrived," Jane added in a quiet voice. "Zeynep took all the ornaments off the fireplace and polished it so it looked lovely. Later in the day, Elizabeth came in from school and was really taken by it. She went straight to it and just stared at it for ages." Jane stopped for a moment and looked at her husband. "Do you want to speak to Elizabeth, or shall I tell you what happened?"

Sarah shook her head. "Please, you go ahead. Elizabeth seemed a little shy when I saw her in the window."

Jane leant over and picked up her cup, took a dainty sip, then returned the cup to the saucer. "Well, Izzy stood in front of the painting for over twenty minutes without speaking. When we managed to tear her away, she told us that she'd felt the warmth of the sun on the back of her neck and that the water of the lake had washed around her feet, caressing them, like a velvet scarf was being pulled across them. She described the garden of the lake house with beautifully coloured roses, and the scent of individual flowers, which lingered in her nostrils. A dark figure at the side of the lake was calling her toward it. It was shouting a name and the words, 'help me' as if it was being hurt in some way." She looked at her husband again and he continued with the story:

"She was totally entranced, we had to pull her away, but once she left the room she said the voice continued. It didn't matter where in the house she was, she couldn't get away from it. After two days I had to take it back, it was driving her crazy."

"Did Elizabeth see the face of the figure?" Sarah asked. "Could she describe it?"

Jane shook her head. "It was faceless, just a grey figure, but Izzy said it seemed sad and lonely."

With not much else to say, they finished their tea and thanked the Owens for their time, along with the tea and biscuits, before going out into the hallway. Elizabeth was standing by the front door. She looked at Sarah as she entered the hallway, her eyes piercing, pupils wide, and in a low voice asked, "Is it you that he's looking for? Are you the Sarah he's trying to reach out to?"

Sarah felt a shiver run down her spine.

"No, Elizabeth, it must be someone else. What makes you think it would be me?"

"He's hurt and alone and searching for Sarah. Your name is Sarah and you've come looking for the painting. It seems logical to me that it's you he's searching for."

Jonathon walked to the door and opened it. "Come on, Sarah. We need to get to the next meeting. Thank you all for your time." Sarah edged passed Elizabeth, whose eyes continued to seem fixated on her.

She got into the car and started to go through everything in her mind: the figure in the painting that she'd bought, as he seemed to be trying to reach out to her, the 'Dream Catcher' painting that Gwyn and Linda took back because Linda was driven insane by the figure constantly calling out to her.

Sarah turned to Jonathon. "Have you still got Gwyn's number? I need to speak to him; I want to know what the figure was saying."

"Sarah," Jonathon answered, matter-of-factly.

"What?"

"That's what he was calling out: Sarah."

"You knew and you didn't tell me. Why didn't you tell me?"

"Well, I didn't think to mention it at the time; it seemed insignificant. I mean, there was no way we could relate it to you; there's thousands of Sarah's out there. It could have been anyone." He pondered for a moment, before adding, "I must admit, though, after hearing what Jane and William have just said, not to mention Elizabeth, I do feel a bit apprehensive about the next meeting. Are you sure you want to go. I could just drive you home, if you want?"

"Just drive," Sarah ordered. "We *have* to go now. I'm in as deep as I could possibly get so let's do it."

They left the town of Knighton and headed toward Malpas and on the way, Jonathon called the second couple again to make sure they were okay to visit.

"Hi, I called earlier. It's Jonathon Ripley, I wanted to speak to you about the painting you returned to Bradley's."

The news wasn't what they wanted to hear. "My wife would prefer not to see you; she'd rather forget about it and move on. If you don't mind."

Sarah interrupted. "Hello, my name's Sarah, it would be really helpful if I could speak with your wife please. It really is very important."

The line went silent for a few moments until he returned to the phone. "Okay," he said, "my wife has changed her mind and says if it's that important to you, she's happy for you to call in."

After hanging up the phone, Sarah sat back in her seat and looked at Jonathon. "Have you any idea what's happening, like, after you'd painted these images, you must have had some kind of idea what was going on?"

He shook his head. "Sarah, I'm sorry, I can't give you an explanation because I have no idea what's going on."

She stared through the passenger side window before turning back to look at him again. "Why did you speak to me at the gallery, there must have been a reason? You don't just walk up to someone the way you did. Why me?"

He sighed. "Like I said at the time, I'd seen you in there before and I wanted to get to know you. There was no reason other than I liked the way you look. I didn't take you to my painting, you chose that yourself and you went back in to buy it without any prompting from me."

Although Sarah wasn't convinced by his answer, she would have to be satisfied with it for now.

CHAPTER **SEVENTEEN**:

They arrived in Malpas after a short journey and Jonathon parked up outside the house.

"Would you like me to go in alone this time?" he asked.

Sarah shook her head. "No, I'll come in. You may not give me the whole story when you come out."

As they were getting out of the car, they noticed someone standing by the gate. "What are their names?" Sarah asked, as she closed the car door.

"Daniel and Kate," he said quietly.

Daniel welcomed them as they approached him at the gate and asked them to be patient with his wife. "She's been through a lot lately, and she can be a bit edgy with people she doesn't know."

"Of course," Jonathon assured him. "If it gets too much for her, we'll leave."

As they entered the house, Daniel guided them through to the kitchen and pulled out a chair for Sarah. Kate was already sitting at the table and smiled at them both.

"I'm Jonathon Ripley and this is my friend, Sarah. We'd just like to ask you a few questions about the painting you returned to Bradley's, if that's okay?"

"Are you the lady that he's looking for?" Kate's words made Sarah and Jonathon reel back in their chairs.

"That who's looking for?" Sarah asked.

"The figure in the painting. He's asked for Sarah. Is it you?"

Sarah offered a friendly smile. "I'm afraid I don't know if it's me or not," she said. "Can you tell me why you returned the painting?"

Kate had a glazed look in her eyes. "That painting is the most beautiful that I've ever seen. Everything about it just entranced me from the moment I laid eyes on it in Bradley's. I bought it and brought it home without even telling Daniel, which I'd never normally do. I never buy on impulse, I'm very careful with our money."

"A bit too careful sometimes," Daniel added with a grin.

"Anyway, when Dan came in from work, I asked him to hang it straight away. It was on this wall behind me. It looked fantastic. That night, I was sitting where you are seated now, and I felt as if I had to get close to it. I needed a closer look. I began to study it up close and I felt as if I was part of it. I was sitting on the bank of the lake with my feet in the water and I could feel the water lapping up against my ankles and calfs. I could also feel the softness of the blades of grass on the back of my thighs as I was sitting there, it was like silk caressing my skin. My senses seemed to be so much more acute, I could hear the frogs croaking, and the crickets stridulating. The smell of wet pine needles and the purest white snow on the tops of the mountains. It was like I was sitting in paradise. Until I looked at the figure." She paused for a moment and inhaled before carrying on. "It was standing upright and staring towards me, but I couldn't make out any features. It was gesturing for me to go to it and calling to me. But when I looked at the reflection in the water, it seemed to be struggling, like it was fighting to get out. I couldn't move to help. I felt like I was nailed to the floor, but it kept calling to me. Eventually, the reflection lay still on the water, and I found myself back in the kitchen." Daniel patted her hand, as though encouraging her to continue. "From that moment, I couldn't get it out of my head. It was like a constant droning. 'Sarah, Sarah, Sarah', over and over in my head. A few days later I went back to the painting, hoping that I'd be drawn in again. Maybe I could stop the voices in my head. Within seconds of facing the painting again I found myself standing in the lake; the water was cold enough to make me take in a few deep breaths. The rough sand under my feet made me adjust my footing so that I didn't fall. As with the first time, the colours and the sounds were intensified, and my senses were amplified." She looked at her husband. "The figure of the man was

109

still lying in the water, which gave me a deeper feeling of sadness than I'd ever felt before."

A silence enveloped the room as Sarah chose her next words carefully. "Did the voice calling *Sarah* stop?" she asked.

Kate shook her head. "No, it was even more intense, like torture, stopping me from sleeping and causing me to suffer migraines like never before. It lasted almost two weeks until I had to give in. I told Dan to take it back. I cried when it went, but it had to go for my sanity."

"If it was causing you so much distress, why did you cry when it was returned?" Sarah asked.

Kate looked down. "I felt my legs while I was sitting on the edge of the lake and I stood up for the first time in over five years after being drawn into the painting that second time."

Kate rolled herself out from under the table and around to where Sarah was sitting.

"I've been paralysed from the waist down since 2004. I haven't been able to feel anything since. But in the painting, I could feel the softness of the grass and the cold water. It was truly magical."

Trying hard to hold back her emotions, Sarah's eyes filled with tears. "That's is the most touching thing I've ever heard. Thank you so much for allowing us to visit and telling us this story."

They got up and Daniel walked them through to the front door where he grabbed Jonathon's hand and shook it. "Thank you with all my heart. Your painting gave Kate a massive lift. She was really down before that, but she's back. Thank you, thank you, so much."

Jonathon and Sarah walked back to the car in disbelief at what they'd just heard. Jonathon opened the passenger door for Sarah and held her arm as she sat down. She still had tears in her eyes.

"You do realise that your paintings are changing lives," she said. "Not just our lives, but it seems like everyone who buys them is affected, some good, some bad, but they're changing lives."

He walked round to the driver's door and got in, then put his hands on the wheel and laid his head on them.

"I can't work out whether that was a good thing or a terrible thing that happened to Kate. She was so happy to have the feeling back in her legs, even for such a short time, but so distraught having to let the painting go."

"Another bittersweet story from one of your paintings. Have you spoken to the last buyers yet?"

Jonathon lifted his head and looked at Sarah. "It's a buyer, not buyers. A lady. I'll try her again now. If I can't get her, we can head that way and stop for a bite to eat while I keep trying."

They set off towards Winsford and Jonathon remembered a lovely place he'd been nearby.

"Have you ever visited Peckforton Castle? I went there once with a friend for afternoon tea, it was excellent. Let's stop there for lunch and then head to Winsford".

Sarah smiled, suddenly starting to feel hungry. "No, I've never been, and yes I'd like to go."

As they drew up to the gates, he turned the car in and drove through an archway on to a single-track lane that led up to the castle. Wide, open fields either side contained grazing sheep, and in the corner of one of the fields was a herd of roe deer, their gracefulness capturing Sarah's gaze as they approached the imposing, sandstone building before them.

Jonathon parked the car and they got out, looking at the beautiful surroundings and taking in the grandeur of the castle and its grounds.

"This is so beautiful," Sarah said. "I can just imagine how it would have been hundreds of years ago, servants running about, horses and carriages. I bet you can see it, too, being an artist. This must be how you get your inspiration."

Jonathon nodded. "It is a magnificent place, I have to say. Come on, let me buy you afternoon tea. I've heard it's pretty spectacular here." He led her along a stone pathway towards the entrance of what appeared to be a restaurant, then placed his hand on the small of her back and guided her through the doors. "After you, m'lady," he said with a bow, and Sarah went inside.

They devoured finger sandwiches and cream cakes, washed down with a large of pot of tea served in delightful, and probably rather expensive china. Then Jonathon paid the bill and went round to Sarah's chair where he bowed again, offering to take her hand. "Shall we?" he said. She slid her chair back and stood up, then followed him outside.

As they began to walk back to the car, they stopped by the chapel that stood in the grounds, and Sarah stumbled slightly, losing her balance on a loose stone. Jonathon reached out to grab her hand, brushing against her gently, until she managed to compose herself. She so wanted to hold onto his hand, but she moved away and continued walking towards the car.

What just happened? Do I have feelings for this man? It was a question she'd thought briefly about before now, but the friendship they'd built was precious to her and she had no intention of spoiling it because of a frivolous crush. Shaking herself off, she decided it would be better not to say anything and perhaps see what came of it, at least until they'd got to the bottom of the mystery of the paintings.

CHAPTER **EIGHTEEN**:

When they got in the car, Jonathon tried the number again for the last buyer. This time she answered.

"Hello?"

"Mrs Eccles?"

"Yes, can I help you?"

"My name is Jonathon Ripley, I'm an artist. I believe you recently owned one of my paintings but returned it to Bradley's?"

"Yes, I did, and if you're calling for me to pay for repairs you can think again. That bloody thing was driving me mad. You're lucky I didn't burn it, never mind return it with a few scratches."

"I'm not calling for repair money, I would simply like to have a chat with you to hear your experience first-hand. I'm only twenty minutes from your house, and I'd like to call in with my companion, Sarah, to speak to you. Would that be okay?"

"Sarah, you say?"

"Yes, Mrs Eccles, she also owns one of my paintings and is very interested to hear why you returned your painting of the lake house?"

"Well, you're more than welcome to call in, but you may not like what I have to say."

"That's okay, thank you, we'll be there shortly."

Sarah glanced at Jonathon. "Sounds like another unhappy customer."

"We'll see when we get there."

Twenty minutes later they arrived at Mrs Eccles' home. The gate was open, so they walked up the path and knocked on the door. Somebody shouted out, telling them to go around the back.

"The gate's open, shut it behind you so the dog doesn't escape."

They walked around the back of the house, where they were greeted by a very large German Shepherd, baring its teeth and growling. They both stopped, frozen to the spot, and looked over at a lady who was sitting on a plastic chair by the patio table. She whistled and the dog instantly laid down and allowed them to walk by, which they did very cautiously.

"Mrs Eccles?"Jonathan asked, still a little perturbed by the dog.

"Yes, that's me," the lady answered. "Don't mind Hannibal; he won't bite you while I'm here."

"Hannibal?" Sarah whispered, though loud enough that Mrs Eccles heard.

"Yes, his name's Hannibal. My late husband named him after the cannibal fella on the telly. Pretty apt really because given the chance he'd probably eat you both."

Sarah didn't really like dogs, especially big angry ones. She'd been bitten as a child by a neighbour's dog and never really took to them after that.

Feeling Sarah's nervousness at the thought of being eaten by a rather aggressive-looking animal, Jonathon began to ask Mrs Eccles about the painting. "What prompted you to buy it?" he asked. "And what made you return it?"

She leaned forward and rested her forearms onto the white plastic table.

"Well," she began, "it all started about ten years ago when my husband was still here."

Jonathon interrupted her. "Erm, just checking. Are we talking about the 'Lake House' painting, because I didn't paint it until a few years ago?"

"Yes, we are. You asked me what prompted me to buy it, so I'm telling you." He cleared his throat, realising this lady wasn't one to be reckoned with. Then she continued her story: "As I was saying, it all started about ten years ago when George was still alive. We went on a fishing trip and stayed in a lovely little cabin by a lake. It was a fantastic location, very similar to your painting. George would go fishing and I would sit and read my books on the terrace outside the front of the cabin. He'd come back later in the day with his catch and I would prepare the fish and cook them. It was heaven. There wasn't a sound other than the birds singing, we never heard a car going by or any of that kind of thing. Perfect peace and quiet for us to pass the day away. Even though we only visited once, it always stuck in our memory."

"Sounds lovely," Sarah said.

"Yeah, we always swore we were going back there at some point, but we never did. George passed away three years ago in July, which left me on my own, except for Hannibal, of course."

She went on to tell them how Hannibal had given her strength after George died and how he'd sat with her every night resting his chin on her knee. "Dogs definitely feel it when their owners pass away; I think they grieve as much as we do."

Jonathon agreed with her. "They're very clever animals," he said, glancing at Hannibal and hoping the dog wasn't going to rest its chin on *his* knee.

Mrs Eccles continued. "Well, a few months ago I went to Bradley's on my way into Crewe and your painting was on the wall. As soon as I saw it, it reminded me of the cabin that George and I had stayed in. I didn't intend to buy a painting that day, I didn't really have room for one, but it brought back the memory so vividly that I had to buy it. I brought it home and looked around for somewhere to hang it until eventually I decided to swap it for the one in the dining room. It was a similar size, so it seemed like the best option."

She told them that it had been Hannibal who took a dislike to it at first. He growled at it and the hairs would raise on the back of his neck, which wasn't really like him. *Not too sure about that*, Sarah thought.

"Anyway, it was probably a day or so later that I sat at the dining table having my dinner and I had a feeling that someone was there, looking over my shoulder, and a bit of a shudder came over me. I looked around and there wasn't anyone there, so I carried on eating when I had the same feeling again. I got up and checked outside, had a walk around, and then stopped by the painting. I looked into it and had this overwhelming urge to move closer. As I got there, the only way that I can describe it is as if I was high on some kind of drug or hallucinogenic. The painting was alive, I could hear bird song like I've never heard it before, I could almost count every leaf on the trees, the snow on the mountains shone like glistening diamonds, and everywhere I looked the colours were incredible. The garden by the cabin was pristine and I could smell every one of the flowers. Paradise isn't a powerful enough word. It was glorious."

"Why would you return it if it was that good?" Jonathon asked.

"Please, allow me to finish, then you'll realise why it had to go. To the side of the cabin there was a grey figure. He had no features to speak of, but I could tell he was sad, his head was low, and his shoulders drooped. And in the water, which was almost glass like, was the reflection of his figure. As I looked at him, he raised his head slightly and asked me to help him and before my eyes the reflection began to thrash about, but the water was still, no movement whatsoever. I looked back at the figure and he said *'help me'* again. The reflected figure thrashed for a minute or so and then stopped and lay still. By this time, I was trying to get myself out of the trance I was in and the figure just repeated time after time the name *Sarah*."

Sarah asked, "Was that the reason you sent it back? Was it because the figure asked for help?"

"No. I sent it back days later. The voice stayed inside my head; it was like a stuck record. It felt like a constantly dripping tap, just eating into my brain. In the end it got so bad that I had to do something to try and stop it but when I tried to stick the scissors through it, it pushed me back. I only managed to scratch it and then I fell back away from it."

Sarah looked shocked. It seemed like everyone who had the paintings had heard the name *Sarah*. Was it really her or could it be another Sarah?

Jonathon stood up. "Thank you for telling us this, Mrs Eccles, we do appreciate your time, but we must be on our way." He held out his hand and Mrs Eccles held out hers, shaking it with a particularly firm grip. Sarah smiled and nodded and thanked her also, then they walked back down the path, passed the huge dog, that now seemed quite settled and not in the least bit scary.

Throughout their journey back to Stokley there was a complete silence. Neither of them could think of anything to say, although they both had so many thoughts bouncing around their heads.

As they pulled into the village Jonathon asked Sarah whether she wanted to go with him the next day to collect the painting. She thought for a while before answering.

"Yes, I'd like to come with you."

He smiled and glanced through his window towards the Lion's Head pub. "Do you fancy a drink before we go home? I can drop the car off at my house and we could walk down."

Without hesitation, Sarah replied, "Yes, why not. We can have a chat about today. It started out as the best day ever, but I now feel like I've been mentally brutalised. A couple of drinks might help to clear my head."

Jonathon dropped Sarah off outside the pub and took his car home. It was only a few minutes' walk away, so Sarah took a seat outside in the beer garden and waited for im.

While she was waiting an older gentleman walked by and stopped. "Sarah? Sarah Pennington? Or Dear Sarah as your father used to call you."

She looked up at the man feeling somewhat confused. "Erm, yes. Do I know you?"

"Peter Kelly. I was a good friend of your father. How are you?"

"I'm fine, still living in Dad's house up on the farm."

"I miss your dad," he said, "though obviously you'll miss him more, but I really miss having the craic with him in here. What happened to Lenny and Tony, I haven't seen them since your dad's funeral. Bit odd really."

"Sorry, I don't think I know them. I didn't know many of Dad's friends."

"Oh, well, they were the two men he went away with to the lake house where he passed away."

"Lake house? I thought they were in a hotel in the Lake District that weekend?"

"No, they stayed in the lake house on the edge of Elswater reservoir."

Sarah sat back in her chair. "Where is the lake house, what area?"

"It's up in the Lake District. One of Lenny's relatives owned it at the time, don't know whether they still do?" Peter smiled and patted Sarah on the shoulder. "Anyway, it was nice bumping into you. Take care of yourself," and with that, he left her to mull over what he'd just told her.

A few minutes went by and Jonathon arrived. "Sorry I took a little bit longer than expected, I had a quick change before I came back."

"Did you see that man I was just talking to as you walked down the road?" Sarah asked.

"Yes, Peter, he comes in here a couple of times a week. Why?"

"Just out of curiosity, where is the lake house that's in your painting?"

"I painted it while I was staying in Windermere in the Lakes. Not too sure about the name of the lake it was actually painted on, though."

"Does the name Elswater, ring a bell?"

"Yeah. That's it, Elswater Lake. How did you know that?"

Sarah told Jonathon what Peter had just said about her dad staying in a lake house in Elswater the weekend that he died. "Tomorrow, when we collect the painting, I'd like to go straight up to Elswater. I want to see it for myself."

"Definitely. We'll go straight there. Do you want me to take you home now?"

"Why would I want to go home?" she asked.

"Well, after the shock of hearing that, you might not be in the mood to stay here anymore."

Sarah laughed. "You must be joking. After the events of today, I reckon we both need a few drinks!"

CHAPTER NINETEEN:

Sarah arrived home in a taxi to a dark house. She paid the driver and asked him if he'd wait while she got in and turned on the lights, to which he agreed then drove off as she waved at him through the window. She then locked the door and sat down in her favourite armchair. She'd had a few drinks and decided itwasn't worth lighting the fire, so she switched on the central heating and went to the kitchen looking for snacks.

Finding a few packets of cheese and onion crisps, she thought about how much she used to enjoy a crisp sandwich. After a few drinks it was always her favourite snack.

She'd had too much to drink, but the wedges of bread thickly coated with butter, and a huge helping of crisps were perfect, and she took the plate through to the living room where she made herself comfy on the couch. *Why don't I have these more often?*

It wasn't long before she fell asleep, the sandwiches half-eaten, and when the plate fell to the floor, she sat up with a start, trying to balance on the edge of the couch to collect the crumbs that were now scattered over the carpet. Giving up, she pulled the throw from the back of the couch and wrapped it around her, snuggling beneath it.

She woke up to the sound of the birds singing and once again, sat up with a start. Inside her head was a drummer pounding away on a big bass drum to no particular tune. She looked at her watch; it was seven-forty in the morning.

Once her eyes could focus, she noticed the spilt crisps spread down her top and all over the couch, and she started to recall how they got there. "Crisp butties, really!" And as she placed her feet onto the floor, she heard a crunching sound and felt the squelch of butter between her toes.

A cup of strong coffee and two paracetomols later, she headed upstairs for a shower, feeling a lot more refreshed afterwards than she had when she woke up earlier on the couch. She dried herself off and got herself dressed, then headed back down to the kitchen.

Hungry now, she filled a bowl with cereal and made another coffee, just as Jonathon pulled up outside. She gestured to him through the window to come in. "I'm not going anywhere until I've eaten this and had another coffee," she said. "Would you like one?"

"Why not, I've already had three, but one more won't hurt."

Shovelling the cereal into her mouth, she asked, "How did I end up in that state last night? I was that bad when I got home that I made myself crisp butties. I haven't had them in years."

"Sound nice, how did they taste?"

"No idea, I ended up wearing them."

They both laughed and drank their coffee while still trying to piece together the previous night, before venturing out to the car.

As Sarah locked the front door, she looked over her shoulder to Jonathon and said, "Let's see what today brings. Hopefully, it's better than yesterday."

They got in the car and set off on their mission to collect the painting from Bradley's in Crewe. Sarah was quite apprehensive and still unsure about it, but she needed to see it after hearing all the stories, and especially after being told that it could be the place where her dad spent his last days. Not only that, but could this person called Sarah, that people had spoken about, actually be her?

She asked Jonathon whether he was nervous about seeing the painting again, but he just shrugged his shoulders, gave a slight shake of his head, and said that he was okay with it.

All the way down to Crewe, Sarah was shuffling about in her seat, picking things up and putting them back, rubbing her hands together and twiddling with the radio controls.

"Sit still, woman, you're going to have a coronary the way you're going."

"How long before we get there?"

"Twenty-five minutes."

"I need the loo. Is there anywhere on the way?"

"We're just coming up to Sandbach services. I'll pull in there and you can run in."

After stopping at the services and Jonathon teasing Sarah about her fidgeting and needing the loo, they finally arrived at Lindsay's, and Jonathon knocked on the door. It was opened almost instantly, and Lindsay passed Jonathon the key. "It's under the tool bench at the back of the garage, feel free to take the sheet it's wrapped in. It came back in that."

He entered the garage and spotted a number of paintings leaning against the walls, two and three deep, but there was only one under the tool bench, and it was wrapped up. He pulled the corner of the sheet back and recognised his work straight away. He covered it up again and closed the garage door before handing the key back to Lindsay.

"Thank you for your help with contacting the buyers, it's very much appreciated."

Lindsay told him that she'd heard the stories first-hand and it sounded to her like they're all a bit nuts. "I've been in this business for a long time and I've never heard so much codswallop to get money back from a seller."

Jonathon was quite happy that she felt that way because it meant that he got the painting back for free.

"Thanks again, Lindsay," he said, before taking it to his car and placing it carefully in the boot.

"Have you had a look at it?" Sarah asked, as he got into the driver's seat.

"Let's stop on the way back and check it's okay," he said.

"Well, we might as well just get it home and we can look at it there," Sarah said in a snappy manner.

Thinking she wanted to go straight to Elswater Lake, he decided to go with her suggestion of going home first and said, "That's fine by me. Home it is then."

On the way back, she fell asleep and began to dream again:

Swimming in the middle of a lake, with the sunshine warming her shoulders and face, she could see all around, it was like a desert landscape; no grass, no trees, just barren land for as far as the eye could see. As she was swimming, she heard somebody calling her name and she began spinning around in the water, looking in every direction, but there wasn't anybody there. She heard her name called again and rotated herself using her hands as paddles.

From beneath the water she felt something against her leg, which prompted her to bring her knees up towards her chest. She was panicking and trying to see down into the water, but it was too murky. Something touched her foot again and she screamed out, her arms flailing as she tried to swim away, but she wasn't moving.

Suddenly, she felt a hand grab a tight hold of her foot. She screamed again and the hand pulled her under...

Jolting forward in the seat, her heart pounding and gasping for breath, she woke up.

"Bloody hell, Sarah, that was a bad dream. You were twitching, fighting with yourself, and making some really weird noises," Jonathon said, touching her arm gently.

"I was in a lake and somebody was trying to pull me under. It was so real."

"Well you're okay, you're still in the car. We're here, anyway." He stopped the car.

"Why are we here?" she asked.

Jonathon looked puzzled. "You said to go home."

"Your home. Not mine. I'm not taking that thing into my house."

He put the car back into gear and set off again, this time to his house. "I thought you meant you wanted to go to your home, not mine."

"Sorry," Sarah said, "I should have been more clear. Let's have a look at the painting when we get to your house, then go up to Elswater before it gets too dark."

When they arrived, he took the painting out of the boot and Sarah followed him inside where he stood it up against a sideboard. He carefully unwrapped it and rested it back against the wall, then turned to look at Sarah. Her eyes were wide, and her jawed had dropped with a look of complete terror on her face.

Scratched into the side of the boat on the lake were the words, *HELP ME, DEAR SARAH*.

"Oh my God!" Sarah exclaimed. "That's what my dad called me. What the hell is happening here? I don't understand. How would Mrs Eccles know he called me that?"

Jonathon placed his arms around her and she reacted by placing her arms around him and pulling him close. For a few seconds they stared into each other's eyes. Sarah wanted to kiss him, but it just didn't seem like the right time. He moved away and led her by the hand. "Come and sit down, I'll make you a drink."

While he was in the kitchen, Sarah went back to the painting. She ran her fingers over the words and felt that pull that she'd felt with the picture in her house, drawing her into it. She could feel the cool water beneath her feet and her senses were heightened just like her previous times.

In what seemed like slow motion, she saw ants marching up the bark of a tree and hear their feet hitting with every step. Just as the others had described, the birdsong was enchanting, and the colours of the sky and the greens of the trees were stunning. She looked towards the cabin and noticed the porch swing was rocking back and forth in the breeze.

She heard voices, not the voices that the others had spoken about, but raised voices, like an argument. Turning to look at the door of the cabin, she saw three men inside. They were shouting and one was becoming really aggressive.

She tried to shout to calm them down, but no words would come.

The door of the cabin opened, and a man backed out. He turned and ran towards the water's edge. As he reached the lake, Sarah caught a glimpse of his face. It was her dad, Gareth. She tried with all her might to shout to him, but she couldn't; she felt paralysed.

In her mind she was screaming at the top of her voice, but her efforts were in vain.

Gareth was standing on the edge of the lake and she could see his reflection in the calm, still waters.

One of the other men threw open the door and bounded out of the cabin; he grabbed the handle from a fishing pole as he scampered across the porch, still ranting and shouting. He ran towards Gareth and took a swipe at his head. Her father reeled back from the glancing blow, and the man swung again. Gareth avoided it this time, but his feet were set in the mud and he fell back into the water, causing a small tidal wave which swept over Sarah's feet.

Sarah screamed at the top her voice, "Daaaad!" But still, no sound emitted from her lips.

He fell backward, his head now under the water. His arms were flailing around, and the water was murky. As his body began to weaken and the flailing slowed, he looked at Sarah, directly at her, and smiled, before taking his last breath.

Sarah had just witnessed her dad's murder by one of the men, and she was completely helpless.

The first man stood over him for what seemed like an age, while he struggled. *Why didn't he help him?*

The second man came out of the cabin and she watched as they pulled Gareth's lifeless body from the lake and laid him on the terrace.

They didn't even try to revive him; they let him die.

She could feel herself fading from the painting and back to reality, before she felt Jonathon's arms around her and heard him say, "Come on, love, sit down, your tea's ready."

She looked at him. "They killed him," she said, so quietly it was almost like a whisper. "The two men murdered my father. I've just seen it all. The Nowhere Man in the painting is my dad and the reflection is where he died." She put her head in her hands and then rubbed her face vigorously. I need to speak to the police; I need to tell them."

"What will you say," Jonathon asked. "You can't tell them you saw him being murdered in a painting, they'll think you're crazy." He sat down on the couch next to her, and placed his arm around her shoulders. "You'll need evidence, Sarah," he added. Then said, "You're in no fit state now, so we'll travel up there in the morning. You need to rest now."

Moving away, he wrapped a coat around her and drove her to back home. "Do you want me to stay with you for a bit?"

She shook her head and went into the house, leaving him feeling helpless as he drove home. The emptiness she now felt inside was exhausting and that night she cried herself to sleep.

CHAPTER **TWENTY**:

S arah was awoken by the sound of her mobile phone ringing. She looked for it but by the time she was able to locate it, it had stopped.

It was starting to go dark outside, so she got up and switched on the light, locked the front door, and drew the curtains. A cup of tea seemed like a nice idea, but as she opened the cupboard to get a cup she stopped. Her body felt weak as she leant against the worktop; even just making a drink was an effort.

Her eyes filled with tears again and she wrapped her arms around herself, while slowly rocking back and forth. She was a complete mess, but she knew that she had to be strong to get justice for her father. *There has to be a way.*

Eventually, she managed to make a cup of tea and took it through to the lounge. Remembering her phone had been ringing earlier, she picked it up and checked who the caller was: Jonathon. She made the decision to ring him back later, not feeling in the mood to chat right now.

Sitting herself down at the dining table, she clenched her cup in both hands and stared into her drink, her mind running in circles. She closed her eyes to think, but the only image she could conjure up was of her dad's lifeless body floating in the lake.

"Where do I even start," she asked out loud. "I don't even know who the two men are, and I have no idea why they'd want to harm my father."

She set her note pad down in front of her and picked up the pen.

Lenny

Tony

What were they shouting at each other?

What did they look like?

The memory was there, but she just couldn't picture them in her mind, frustrated with herself because she knew she'd seen their faces in that picture.

Peter – visits the Lion's Head, might know where Lenny and Tony are – ask him for their surnames

Kate, Elizabeth, Mrs Eccles – did they hear anything, did they see anything that they forgot to mention?

It was like she knew there was something missing, but she couldn't remember…

Then, it suddenly dawned on her! *When did Jonathon paint the scene? Was he there at the time? Did he actually witness the murder?*

She was now reaching a point where she began to question her own sanity. Maybe it *was* a dream. *Was that possible? Could I have dreamt that I'd seen the crime?*

Within an hour, Sarah had a list of names, dates, thoughts, and questions. She tore off the top page and started again, deciphering the important parts and disregarding any parts that she felt weren't significant.

Question Jonathon about dates, she added to her list.

Unable to think anymore, she eventually went to bed, a thousand thoughts swimming around in her head, before she gradually fell asleep.

It was three-am when she woke, and the room was dark with just the light from the hallway seeping in through the slightly open door. She lay on the bed for a while and then had a thought: *What if I look into the painting? The figure has been trying to communicate; could it be that it's trying to tell me about Dad?*

Rushing down the stairs she went straight to the painting and stared at it, but nothing happened. She leant as close as she could and continue to stare, but still, nothing. The tip of her nose was even resting against the it and in her mind, she was begging to be let in.

Then, as she moved away, the scent of wet pine filled her nostrils and she began to hear the rustling of the trees. Suddenly, she was standing in the clearing, and when she looked around, the figure was much clearer, although still quite blurred. Sarah could make out more of the features and recognised it. It was definitely her father. She tried to speak to him but, as had happened previously, the sounds just wouldn't come.

He was looking at her now, and she could make out tears in his eyes. He reached out as if wanting to hold her hand, but she couldn't move. *I saw them do it, but I need your help* It was as though her mouth was sealed shut. Frustration once more enveloped her and she raised her hand to wave, but as she did, the figure started to fade away.

Don't go, stay with me.

It was still only four thirty, but Sarah was bursting at the seams to begin her search for the truth. She opened up her laptop and typed in the address bar: Gareth Pennington. Unfortunately, there were many and so she began thinking of ways to narrow it down. Gareth Pennington, Stokley. Then, Gareth Pennington, 26th May 1953.

This brought up his Facebook and Twitter accounts as well as the obituaries in the local newspaper following his death. She clicked on the obituaries and began to read through them, mostly from friends, and, surprisingly, one from her auntie Karen and Colin.

There was also one from Lenny and Sue:*Missing my best mate, big G, you're at rest now with your darling Carol, RIP mate xxx.* Seeing the one from Lenny prompted her to look for another one from someone named Tony, but no avail. She read through Lenny's again. It didn't seem like the message that someone who'd murdered him would write, but then she'd never seen one from a murderer, so she couldn't know.

Clicking on to her dad's Facebook profile, which she had memorised when he passed away, she began to scroll through his friends list to find anyone called Tony or Lenny, and within a few seconds, she found *Lenny Roberts* and clicked on his profile. A short stubby man with a bald head popped up on her screen and she wracked her brain to remember the men she'd seen murder her father, almost certain they were tall, slim men.

She scrolled through Lenny's Facebook page to the time Gareth had died, noticing lots of photographs that he'd shared from fishing and golfing trips they'd been on together. Looking at the posts, it looked like he was devastated by Gareth's death, which made her think that he wasn't the person she was looking for. She clicked back to his profile and sent him a friend request. *It can't hurt; at least then I can ask him some questions.*

Going back to her dad's account she scrolled through for *Tony*, but couldn't find him. She then typed in *Anthony,* and again scrolled through. It seemed odd that he went on a trip with two men but one of them had no links to her dad and didn't post an obituary.

She clicked onto his Twitter account next, but then remembered she'd deactivated the account after he'd died.

Back in the Google address bar, Sarah continued to search, and came across a local newspaper clip about the dispute over the land that she now owned. The dispute had been filed by a local builder who had applied for access to his land behind her house, through what were now her fields.

She opened it up. A photograph of her dad jumped onto the screen, standing on the road behind the house, a headline above his head reading: *Farmer says "No" to housing development.*

After Gareth's death, Sarah had been approached by a construction company wanting to buy the land to gain access to the fields behind, which were landlocked by hers. She had contemplated selling but wasn't impressed with the offer or the attitude of the man wanting to buy it, so despite numerous calls from the company, some of which became quite offensive, and a couple of strongly worded letters through the door, which she threw onto the fire, she decided to lease it to tenants instead. For a few months after it was leased, she'd continued to receive calls from unknown numbers, some of them abusive. It was a memory she wanted to put behind her, but suspected there could be more going on with that company and her dad's wishes than she'd first thought.

She began to read through the story. It *was* the same company that had approached her. They were looking to build a new housing estate on the land, and the article reported that Gareth had prevented that happening. The builder had hoped to secure himself a million-pound deal, and this information sent a shiver down her spine as she started to wonder if this was the reason her beloved dad had been killed.

Taking a few more notes and hoping Lenny might accept her friend request, she printed out the news article and decided to wait until morning when she would go to the place Gareth's photo had been taken. *Something's not right...*

CHAPTER **TWENTY-ONE**:

At the first sign of light shining through the gaps in the curtains, Sarah grabbed her coat and made her way to the very spot her dad had stood for the journalist's article. She climbed over the small sandstone wall and walked along the edge of the field until she reached the neighbour's land. Sure enough, that was the shortest route from the road to the adjacent field.

The neighbours still farmed their land, so it didn't make much sense for anyone other than the farmer to need access to it, but she was determined to find out more about the article.

On the walk back down to her house, she called Jonathon. "I think I might have stumbled across something when I was searching through Dad's history. Something that might give a reason to murder him."

"Oh?" Jonathon said. "I'll be over in twenty minutes; put the kettle on and we can run through everything."

By the time Sarah got back to the house she noticed that Lenny had accepted Facebook friend request. She rushed through, flicked the kettle on and set up the cups ready for Jonathon to arrive and then plonked herself down at the table and began to message Lenny.

Hi Lenny, I'm Gareth Pennington's daughter, Sarah. I know it's been a while, but I'd like to speak to you about my father's death. Could you please call me on the number in my profile?

Just as she hit 'send', there was a knock at the door. Jonathon was standing in the porch. "Come in, the kettle's boiled and the cups are ready. Feel free to make some toast if you're hungry."

While he was making the tea, Sarah entered the name of the construction company: *Shawcross Developments*. It seemed to be a small development company with a few local, modest housing schemes. Then, she checked on Companies House and found three Directors: Shaun Shawcross, Beverly Shawcross and Anthony Shawcross. *Bingo, there's Tony.* She added their phone number to the list in her notebook, knowing she needed to have more evidence than just a name and the fact she'd seen something while inside a painting.

Jonathon came through with the tea some toast and sat down at the table. "So, Mrs Holmes, are you going to tell me what you've found?"

"Mrs Holmes, who's that?"

"The wife of Sherlock," he said, with a grin.

Sarah rolled her eyes and tutted a few times. "Okay, I woke up early hours this morning and decided to do some delving. I started by listing all the things I already knew and the people I'd already spoken to. Once I had a list I went on the internet and searched my dad's name, the area, and his date of birth. The obituaries brought up a message from a Lenny Roberts, but nothing from Tony, who is the other person I knew was with my dad at the cabin. Given that Tony was supposed to be a friend, that seemed a bit odd, so I clicked on Dad's Facebook account and checked through his friends. I found Lenny, but there wasn't a Tony on the list.

Jonathon butted in. "Couldn't Tony be known as Anthony?"

"I also checked and there wasn't an Anthony either. After checking through Lenny's friends for a Tony, or Anthony, I sent Lenny a friend request so that I could then private message him, which I've done, and I'm waiting for a call off him."

"Why would you message Lenny? He might be one of the men who murdered your dad."

Sarah shook her head and said, "No, I don't think he is. He was devastated by my dad's death and he's a short, stout man. The men I saw were taller and thinner. Anyway," she continued, "after checking Dad and Lenny's Facebook pages, I found a newspaper article with a picture of Dad. He was stopping a construction company known as Shawcross Developments, from gaining access through our land to build a housing development. It must have cost them a fortune, and they obviously lost the contract." Jonathan munched on the toast, urging her to carry on. "So, then I discovered who the managing director of Shawcross Developments is."

"And?" he asked, holding the toast midway from the plate to his mouth.

"None other than someone called Anthony Shawcross." She smiled and tapped her pen on the notebook in front of her. "Shawcross approached me after Dad died, hounding me to buy the land. They even sent several abusive letters hoping I'd cave in."

Jonathon threw the toast into his mouth, chewed it, then swallowed it down. Then, he leaned back in his chair and folded his arms. "You've certainly done your homework Mrs Holmes. I'm really impressed. But aren't you going to need more than just the fact his name is Tony and that he wanted to buy the land to nail him?"

"Yes, I am," she said, nodding frantically. "Drink up, we're going to Culshaw's farm to speak to Mr Culshaw. We need to find out what happened and more about his dealings with Shawcross."

"Where's Culshaw's farm?"

"It's the farmland that Shawcross was trying to gain access to, on the other side of mine. Without access it's landlocked."

They hurried down their tea and set off on the five-minute drive to Culshaw's farm. As they made their way through the gates in front of the farmhouse, there was a tall, stocky man getting into a Jeep. Looking like he was in his late seventies, he wore a checked cap and a green tweed shooting jacket. He stopped and looked over to their car as they were getting out of it. "Can I help you folks?"

"Hi. I'm Sarah. Gareth Pennington's daughter. I own the farm and land next door to you."

Mr Culshaw gave them a look that could kill. "Unless you've come to offer me some compensation, you can piss off."

Sarah stopped in her tracks. "I'm sorry. I don't think we've met. Have I upset you in some way?"

"No, you haven't, but your father did so I'd appreciate it if you left, before I say something I'll regret."

Taken aback by the hatred he seemed to have for her, even though they'd never met or even crossed paths before, Sarah went on to ask, "Could I just ask a few questions about Shawcross before I go?"

The man scoffed. "I'm surprised you've got the nerve to ask after what your father did."

"If you'll allow me to explain, you might think differently. I think they murdered my dad because he wouldn't sell them the land."

Mr Culshaw shook his head and laughed. "I've known them most of my life, they wouldn't hurt anyone. They can be a bit pushy when they want something, but they don't need this land to build on, they've got the money to buy whatever land they want. They're definitely not murderers. I think you're barking up the wrong tree."

"I thought they'd have lost a fortune by not getting access. Surely they'd be a bit angry over that?" Sarah suggested.

Mr Culshaw shook his head again. "If anyone lost a fortune it was me."

It suddenly entered Sarah's head that Mr Culshaw was a similar size to the man who took a swing at her dad. "Mr Culshaw, do you mind if I ask your first name."

"You certainly want your penny's worth of questions don't you. My name is George, if that helps."

Thanking him, Sarah got back into the car and told Jonathon to take her home. If what Mr Culshaw had said about Shawcross was right, and they wouldn't hurt anyone, she was right back at the beginning.

Back at the house, Sarah reviewed her notes, turning to Jonathon "What now?" she asked.

Jonathon shrugged. "Well, you haven't actually spoken to anyone at Shawcross to rule them out. Why don't we start there? Call Anthony Shawcross and ask for a meeting."

Sarah picked up her phone and dialed the number for Shawcross Developments,asking to be put through to Anthony Shawcross when a lady answered.

There was a short delay before the lady asked, "May I ask what it's regarding, please?"

"It's a personal matter," Sarah said, rather haughily. "Can you tell him it's Sarah Pennington from Pennington's farm?"

The line went quiet for a few moments, then, "Anthony speaking, are you calling with good news. Have you decided to sell?"

"Well, er, no actually. I'm calling about my dad's murder."

"Murder? I thought he died in an accident?"

"Some new information has come to light and it seems that the accident wasn't so accidental after all."

Anthony went silent for a few seconds and then said, "Bloody hell, that's a hell of a shock. Is there anything I can do?"

Sarah hesitated. "I'm ringing to see whether you had anything to do with his death, or if you may know anything that might help me find his killer."

"Sorry, are you saying you think I had something to do with it? Certainly not. What would make you think that I could do anything like that?"

Sarah started to cry at that point, unable to cope with anymore bad news. "I'm sorry, but I have to start somewhere and there was a motive for you to have done it. You wanted the land, and you made all those nasty telephone calls."

Anthony's voice softened. "I understand, Sarah, but you're way off the mark asking me. We had a bit of an argument over it, granted, but we shook hands and moved on. We took the offer for Culshaw's land off the table and bought other land in Calsden, where we actually made more profit than we'd forecasted to earn on that site. I had no hard feelings towards Gareth at all, and I certainly never made any nasty telephone calls."

Sarah put the phone down and slumped back in her seat, realising she'd exhausted the two main leads that she had.

Jonathon began reading through her notes. "What's this?" he asked, a shocked expression on his face. "You think I had something to do with it? You've got a note here to check dates with me and whether I was a witness. Sarah, why would you think such a thing after I've helped you as much as I have?"

Wiping the tears from her eyes, she looked up at him. "I'm sorry, Jonathon, I just jotted down everything that had gone on, and because you did the painting and we later found out that the figure was my dad, it just got me thinking. But, while we're talking about it, do you remember what date you painted it?"

Jonathon got up, headed to the front door, and opened it.

"Where are you going?" she asked.

"Home, I can't believe you thought I had anything to do with this, I'm going home to think. I'll check the date on the back of the painting and text it to you."

This is going from bad to worse.

Twenty minutes later, Sarah received a text from Jonathon:

25th Aug 2017

Thank you, and I'm sorry, she wrote back.

Just as she about to put her phone on the table, it rang. It was a number she didn't recognise. "Hello?"

"Hi, Sarah. It's Lenny, Lenny Roberts. Gareth's friend. You sent me a message to call you."

Surprised to hear his voice, she said, "Lenny, thank you so much for calling me. I'm sorry for bothering you after all this time. Are you okay?"

"Yeah, I'm fine, love. A bit shocked to hear from you but glad that I have. Is there something you needed me for?"

"The thing is," Sarah began, "it's come to light that my dad's death could have been deliberate." A pause, then, "I wanted to ask you what happened on that day."

Lenny half sniggered. "You're serious, aren't you?"

"Yes, one hundred per cent serious. Can you run me through what you remember from the day, please?"

"No problem. Erm. We got up that day and had a full cooked breakfast because we were planning to be out on the boat all day fishing. After breakfast, we got our tackle together and I went to get some beers from the fridge to stock up the cooler box, but there was only a couple left so Tony asked me if I'd go and get some. The nearest shop was miles away in a village, so I grabbed the keys, jumped in the car and left."

"Did you go alone?" Sarah asked.

"Yes. It was about a forty-minute round trip. I stopped for fuel on the way back to save us stopping on our way home the next day and then when I got back to the cabin, Tony was frantic."

"What do you mean, frantic?"

"Well, he was shouting, 'I think he's dead, call an ambulance, I think Gareth's dead', and I ran over to see what was going on."

"And what happened next?"

"Well, I called for an ambulance while Tony was trying resuscitate Gareth. He said he was in the cabin and when he came out, Gareth was lying on his back in the lake. Said he'd got his feet stuck in the mud and fell in. I helped to try and revive him, but..."

"But what?" Sarah asked, tears welling up in her eyes now.

"He was gone, love. I tried my best, I really did, but it was too late. I'm sorry, Sarah." Then he began to cry, making Sarah feel a little awkward, and she began to cry, too.

Sarah was first to speak a few seconds later. "Do you remember anything else about the day, anything that didn't seem right, that you may not have thought was significant at the time."

Lenny seemed to compose himself and said, "No, there wasn't anything. Well, there was a car parked half-way down the road to the cabin, which was a bit odd because the only thing at the bottom of the road was the cabin. I just thought maybe someone was fishing."

Sarah sat up straight in her chair. "What kind of a car was it?" she asked.

"A blue Ford, like a Fiesta or a Focus. Light blue."

Sarah made a note. Did you get the registration number?"

"I'm sorry, love, I didn't notice it. But it looked like a fairly new car, if that helps."

"Lenny, do you know Tony's surname?"

Lenny thought for a few moments. "I can't remember it, to be honest. That weekend at the cabin was the first time I met him."

"Did he have any distinguishing features or was there anything else that you can remember about him?"

Lenny thought again, then said. "His dad owned the farm next to yours."

"Culshaw's farm?"

"Yes. That's him, Culshaw. Tony Culshaw."

"Are you sure that's his name?"

"Yes definitely, Tony Culshaw."

Am I finally getting somewhere? Sarah thanked Lenny for all his help and put the phone down before she rang Jonathon.

"Hello." His voice was quite abrupt, but Sarah chose to ignore.

"Got him," she said.

"Good for you, it wasn't me, then?"

"Jonny boy, I'm really sorry. I need you to come back so that we can hatch a plan to snare him."

After a lot of grovelling and persuading him to come back, Jonathon arrived at Sarah's and she told him about the conversation with Lenny.

"Do you have any idea who the blue car belonged to?" Jonathon asked.

"Not a clue, but we've got the advantage of knowing there *was* a blue car,*and* we have an approximate model."

CHAPTER
TWENTY-TWO:

After a brief phone call to Anthony Shawcross after their conversation the previous day, the next morning they made their way to Shawcross Developments where Anthony had agreed to meet them. A well-dressed lady showed them to a meeting room on the first floor and offered them drinks, to which they nodded and accepted.

"Posh, isn't it?" Jonathon said, looking around the room when the lady had gone.

"It is. I was frightened to sit down in case the leather chair got damaged!"

The lady arrived back shortly after and placed a tray of steaming cups on the table, setting them down on coasters containing the Shawcross Developments company logo. They sat in silence for a few minutes until the door opened, and in walked an elderly gentleman in golf attire and a cap. He removed his cap and offered his hand to them both. "Anthony Shawcross," he said. "How can I be of assistance?"

"I hope we're not interrupting your game of golf," Sarah said, shaking his hand. "Shall we come back another time?"

He shook his head and sat down. "No, I don't tee off until ten, but it's too far to be going home to change so I thought I'd wear my golfing clothes to save time."

Sarah began to explain her theory to Anthony Shawcross and tried, in the best way possible, to tell him how she'd found out her dad was murdered, realising it probably made her sound like a complete nutcase!

Anthony listened, averting his eyes from her to Jonathon and back again, as she told him what she'd learned from Lenny. "I spoke to George Culshaw also; he wasn't happy with Dad, but he didn't strike me as a killer."

Anthony nodded occasionally, taking sips of his tea. When she got to the part about the blue Ford parked on the road to the cabin, he stopped her.

"Did you know that Tony has a brother?"

Sarah looked at Jonathon, who shrugged. "No, I hadn't thought of a brother,"she said, "but I guess that would make sense."

"His brother's name is Terence. He's not the sharpest knife in the drawer and follows Tony around like a lap dog. The reason I mention him is because he owns a light blue Ford Focus."

"That would fill in the blanks," Jonathon said, looking at Sarah, "but murder seems extreme over your dad not allowing access to their land."

Anthony nodded and began to wrap his fingers on the tabletop. "It seems extreme until you put one-point-six-million pounds into the mix. George is getting on a bit and I'm sure Tony would have been really pissed off when that deal was falling through. Maybe he tried to talk Gareth round, and when he couldn't, decided if he were out of the way that you would sell."

Sarah and Jonathon nodded. It did seem like a plausible motive to kill.

Anthony stood up. "Anyway, I do need to leave, I'm afraid, I have to get to the golf course." Then he started walking to the door and turned back to face them both. "If you need anything, I'm here to help if I can," he added, smiling before opening the door and leaving them in the meeting room alone.

After they finished their tea, they stood up and left the room, making their way back to the car.

"So," Sarah began, "it seems like we now have the killer. We also have his accomplice along with a substantial money motive."

Jonathon agreed and started up the car. "We should now go and see Lenny and ask him to identify Tony, Terence, and Terence's car. Come on," he said, then put it in gear and set off.

It didn't take long to get to Lenny's house, and he opened the door as they got out of the car and smiled at Sarah, who recognised him straight away from her dad's funeral. "You don't look anything like your Facebook profile," she said. "I wouldn't have known you from that, but I remember you and your wife now that I've met you again in real life. Lovely to see you."

Lenny took them into the lounge; a cosy room with a three-piece suite and a display cabinet containing trophies and ornaments and a large collection of crystal glasses. They sat down on the comfy sofa and Sarah started to tell him how they'd met Anthony Shawcross and might be able to get him to help them with their plan to catch Garenth's killer.

"How do you know what happened that day," Lenny asked Sarah, who looked at Jonathon, realising she needed to find the right words to make this sound more realistic than it probably would.

"Okay, I know this might sound weird," she began, "but it was like a vision I had. It was so vivid, so much so that it led me to investigate it to this extent."

"Did you see their faces in your vision?" he asked.

Sarah shook her head sadly. "No, I didn't. That's why we're here, to see if you can identify them as the two people I saw, and whether you can identify the car?"

Lenny put his head down and clenched his hands together tightly. "I'm not sure that I can do that. What if it wasn't them? What if you're wrong?" he said. "The car could have belonged to anyone. I don't want to be a part of putting two innocent men behind bars."

Sarah sat forward. "Lenny, we have the motive, and with your help we can have them charged with the murder of my dad. He was your best friend. Please, help me do this for my dad."

Lenny took a deep breath and started to rub the back of his neck. "I'm sorry, Sarah, I can't. You'll have to find another way."

Sarah and Jonathon were both stunned into silence. Realising they were getting nowhere, they got up and started walking to the door. Then Sarah turned to Lenny with tears rolling down her cheeks. "A friend in need, eh?" she said, before she scoffed and left the house.

On the way home, Sarah asked Jonathon if they could go to his house first as she wanted to see the painting again. Agreeing, he pulled up outside his home and led her inside.

"Would you mind leaving me alone for a little while?" she asked. "I want to be alone with the painting." He nodded his head and went into the kitchen.

Sarah stood in front of it, her eyes filled with tears. "I tried Dad, I really tried, but things are against me at every turn."

And before she knew what was happening, once again, she found herself being drawn into it, feeling the water lapping up against her legs. She lifted her tear-filled eyes to where her dad lay the last time she was there. The two men were there, looking over his lifeless body, and she tried again to shout.

The man who attacked Gareth put the fishing pole handle underneath the veranda of the cabin and gave it a kick. Then, while she watched the two men walk toward the cabin door, she saw a third man through the window. Her eyes opened wide and she wiped away the tears that were blurring them. The third man was Lenny; he'd been there all along. He hadn't left for beer as he'd said.

She held her breath and listened, straining her ears, hoping not to miss a word. She could hear them talking about calling the ambulance and Lenny said to leave it for five minutes to make sure he was dead.

"This is the easiest hundred grand I'll ever earn," he was saying. *"You two just need to get Shawcross to convince Gareth's girl to sell up. It shouldn't be that hard to convince her and if she won't sell, maybe you could pay her a visit."*

Sarah tried to shout at him, "Bastard," but once again, the word wouldn't emit from her mouth. Then she found herself standing in front of the painting again.

"JONATHON!" she shouted.

"What is it?" he said, running from the kitchen to stand next to her.

"He was part of it! Lenny was part of it! He let them murder his best friend, my dad, for a hundred grand. That's why he wouldn't help. If we got them, they'd have given him up." She sat back on the edge of the table and stared at the painting. "I swear I'm going to get them Dad. They won't get away with this, I promise."

CHAPTER
TWENTY-THREE:

The next day, Sarah called Anthony Shawcross to ask if he'd meet them again, to which he agreed. She turned up at his office a short while later and explained what had happened, trying to put her story to him without it sounding like she was losing her mind.

"I need your help," she said. "I have no real evidence to prove any of this, but I'd like to make Tony believe that the sale may be back on. It might make him do something to try to force it through."

Anthony asked Sarah to go over her vision again. "You saw Tony throw the fishing pole under the veranda. You're certain of that?" he said.

"Yes, he kicked it further under. Why?"

He thought for a minute. "Why don't you see if you can get it? If you're right, and he hit your dad with it, there'll be DNA from your dad's head wound, and Tony's fingerprints will be on it."

Sarah jumped up and hugged Anthony, much to his surprise. "Oh my God, that's the evidence I need. You're a genius."

After leaving the Shawcross offices, she began to walk through the village, and on the way, she stopped at the police station.

"How can I help you?" the desk officer asked.

"I'd like to speak to someone about a murder that was never reported," she said, a determined tone prompting the officer to tell her to take a seat while he called a police constable to come down.

144

Five minutes went by and a smartly-dressed female police officer approached her. "Can I help?" she said. "I'm Constable Jennings."

"I need to report a murder," Sarah said.

Jennings looked at her then said, "Okay, let's go somewhere more private. Please, follow me," before leading Sarah to an interview room. They sat down opposite each other at a small desk. "So, before we begin, what's your name?"

"Sarah Pennington," she answered. "You're going to need a large notepad and pen as this is going to be a long and slightly weird afternoon."

Sarah started at the beginning and worked her way through all the ghostly stuff, all the spooky stuff, and all the people along the way, and a few hours later she was at the point where she entered the painting for the last time. "I saw the whole thing and I heard every word. I know how crazy this sounds but, if you want to call Jacob, Kate, Elizabeth, or Mrs Eccles, I'm certain they'll verify everything I've told you, one hundred and ten per cent."

Officer Jennings observed Sarah throughout her explanation like she was an absolute fruit cake. "So, you want me to believe that you, and a number of other people, float in and out of paintings, and there are scary figures in these paintings that turn out to be your father, who happens to be murdered while you watch, and the men who did it confess right in front of you?"

Sarah sat back in the chair. "I know it sounds a bit fantasy, goblins and ghouls' stuff, but if you can give me a few hours of your time tomorrow, I'll prove it to you. We can go up to the lake house and I'll show you where he hid the weapon. You'll have my dad's DNA and Tony Culshaw's fingerprints on the handle. I'm going to organise a meeting with Shawcross Construction, The Culshaws and myself to sign for the sale of the land. I'll wear a wire and try to get more information out of Tony about the trip."

Officer Jennings got up from her chair and walked around the desk, leaning with both hands on it next to Sarah. "You're either a complete and utter nutjob or I'm the one missing a couple of marbles, but either way, I'm in," she said, much to Sarah's surprise. "I can't miss this one on my C.V. I'll get an officer from the Cumbria Constabulary to call at the lake house and hopefully recover the fishing pole, and if it's there, we can look into the incident."

"Thank you," Sarah said, delighted.

"I'm not promising anything. We can't prosecute him on a dream and such a small amount of evidence, but, if it's there, it'll give us a starting point."

That night, Sarah called Anthony Shawcross and explained that she'd been to the police and was going to need more evidence if they were going to catch Tony and Terence. She asked if he would help.

With a bit of persuasion, Anthony agreed. "If it means getting to bottom of this mystery, I'm in," he said.

"Would you mind calling Mr Culshaw and inviting him and Tony to a meeting with us both so we can discuss the sale of the land? The police have agreed to let me wear a wire and record what they have to say. We're hoping Tony might trip himself up about the day's events."

"Leave it with me," Anthony said.

The next morning, Sarah called the police station to enquire about the fishing pole handle.

Officer Jennings picked up the phone and said, "We found it, it's on its way to us now. We'll get it to forensics for checking, but we won't hear back for a day or two."

Sarah gave out a little screech and asked if she could see it, or better still, get a photograph of it.

"We can't allow that," Jennings said. "Why do you need to see it?"

"I'd like to get one the same if possible, I have a plan. I suppose if I had the make, or model and colour, that would help."

Officer Jennings eventually agreed to give her that information, saying she understood, and Sarah then spent the next few hours meticulously setting out her plan for the meeting. She would have to make Tony feel at ease and then bring up the death of her dad, hopefully to get him talking about the day. The story that Lenny had told her could perhaps be cross referenced with Tony's story and might just trip him up.

While she was planning, her mobile rang. It was Jonathon asking whether she fancied a bite to eat in the village café.

"Yes, I'd love to," she said, "and I've made a bit of progress. I might need your help if you don't mind. I'll meet you there in half an hour."

Sitting in the café, Sarah explained her plan. "I've been to the police and they've retrieved the fishing pole. I'm waiting for Officer Jennings to let me know the make of it so I can see whether I can get one the same to take with me for the meeting. I'll be wearing a wire to recordwhat he says, and hopefully he'll say something to incriminate himself." She kicked him under the table. "Have you heard a word I've said or is your phone more important?"

Jonathon placed his phone down on the table and raised his eyes with a worried look on his face. "Are you sure you want to be in a room with a suspected murderer and make him nervous? If he's killed once, there's no saying he won't do it again."

"He's not going to do anything with Anthony and you in the room, is he?"

Jonathon's expression changed to a look of shock. "I'm going to this meeting? When did I agree to that?"

"You wouldn't let me go there alone, would you?" she said, smiling sweetly. "After all that we've been through to get the paintings and find the truth, you have to come."

Pondering for a few moments, Jonathon finally agreed to go, and Sarah told him her plan of action.

Just as they were finishing their meal, Sarah's phone rang.

"It's Officer Jennings. The fishing pole is here. I'd like you to call into the police station so we can discuss our next move."

CHAPTER
TWENTY-FOUR:

"**A**re you sure about this, Sarah," Jennings asked as they sat in a meeting room at the station." Are you absolutely happy with meeting Tony Culshaw and wearing a wire?"

"I'm a bit nervous," Sarah replied.

"We'll have officers nearby, just in case they're needed, but I want you to be sure you're happy about going ahead with it," Jennings reiterated.

"Yes, I'll be okay. Jonathon and Anthony will be there as well as the police listening in."

"I'll be visiting Anthony Shawcross to fill him in on what's going on. We don't want him mentioning anything that might impact on the case."

As they stood up to leave, Officer Jennings gave Sarah a slip of paper containing the details of the rod, as well as her direct contact number.

"It's a retractable pole. There was trace evidence on the end of it, hopefully enough to get your dad's DNA, but I won't know until tomorrow. If you want to organise your meeting for the following day, we'll know exactly what we've got on him by then."

Sarah and Jonathon headed back to Sarah's house, but she was starting to feel the strain of the whole thing.

"Would you come in for coffee?" she asked. He nodded and turned the car engine off.

Would this be a good time to tell him about her feelings for him? After all, the hunt was nearly over, and it couldn't do any harm. She mulled it over and decided that tonight would be the night.

When they got inside the house, Jonathon suggested they have something a bit stronger. "A glass or two of wine, what do you think?"

"Sounds like a plan, Johny boy."

They moved into the garden where they opened a bottle of red wine, before settling down on the patio settee to watch the sunset. Feeling relaxed and confident, Jonathon's phone suddenly began to ring and he deleted the call without answering.

"Bloody sales calls, they're a pain," he said, before putting it in his pocket. "A toast," he added, "to Sarah Holmes."

It was a few bottles later whilst watching the sun go down over the fields, that it started to rain quite heavily, so they moved inside. Sarah went to the bathroom to freshen up. As she was swilling water over her face she looked up at the mirror and in the reflection was her dad, looking over her shoulder with a beaming smile on his face. She swiftly turned around to see him, but the room was empty. Quickly looking back to the mirror to try to catch another glimpse, she started to cry. The stress of it all was getting to her. "Oh, Dad, I'll be glad when this is all over and you can rest in peace. I'm doing the best I can, we're going to get him."

"I love you," she suddenly heard, in a whispered voice, and once again, she turned around to find an empty room.

"I love you too, Dad."

She then opened the bathroom cabinet and took out her favourite perfume, sprayed a little on her neck, applied a little lipstick, and brushed her hair. After checking her reflexion in the mirror and telling herself she looked good, she winked and said, "Here's looking at you, kid," before making her way downstairs to tell Jonathon about her feelings for him. In the back of her mind she was worried that he might not be expecting it, but she was quietly confident that he felt the same way.

As she reached the top of the stairs, she heard faint voices, and stopped for a few seconds, listening intently; Jonathon was talking to someone. She stooped down to look into the living room, and could just see the legs of him and another man. Slowly bending her knees, she saw the back of the other man, dressed in a green army jacket and jeans. She knew that the next step creaked, so she had to strain to see more without moving her feet.

Almost in a crouched position now, she saw the person that Jonathon was talking to; it was Tony Culshaw. They were shaking hands and whispering and she heard Jonathon say that Sarah was upstairs, that she'd had a few drinks and was probably asleep.

What's Jonathon doing? Why is Tony Culshaw here?

Then, it suddenly dawned on her that he'd been texting all evening. Was he in on it?

Backing up the stairs, desperately avoiding the creaking steps and floorboards, she arrived at her room and locked the door, her mind racing. *Was Jonathon in it from the start?* Had he duped her all along? She'd told him all her plans to oust Tony and, worst of all, she was about to open her heart to him.

She looked around for her mobile, realising she'd left it on the table in the garden. Panic started to fill her mind as she recalled how she'd sneak out through the spare bedroom window when she was a child, dropping on to the shed and into the garden. *Maybe I can do that?*

Tentatively, she opened the door and began to navigate the landing, avoiding the creaky sections, knowing each step could alert them; every move could be fatal. As she reached the top of the stairs, she looked left toward the spare bedroom door, noticing it slightly ajar, which was a relief because it had a handle that made a loud clicking sound when it was opened.

As she turned at the top of the landing, she heard the creak of the bottom stair. Her heartbeat multiplied as the panic set in again. She leant back against the landing wall, and edged her way along, trying to avoid being seen as they came up the stairs.

"Dad, please help me, I know you're here," she mouthed, finally managing to reach the bedroom, easing her way in and quietly pushing the door almost closed behind her. Then, she turned towards the window and let out a deafening scream as her heart sank in her chest.

Jonathon was sitting on the window ledge, grinning at her with a devilish look in his eyes. It was like a scene from a horror movie, his silhouette against the window with the rain beating against it and the darkened clouds enveloping his shape.

Sarah leaned back against the door as if defeated. "Why?" she said. "I trusted you. I was about to tell you I love you. What the fuck are you doing?."

He shrugged his shoulders. "I got a call from Tony a few days ago. He'd seen us together around the village and asked if I would have a word with you about selling the land. At first, I refused, but he rang me again this morning with an offer I couldn't refuse; I told you that I'd win the lottery or something and here it is. You need to understand, there's no money in sketching and book covers, and I'm in a lot of debt."

Sarah glared at him and shook her head. "You sold me out, for a few quid?"

"It's okay for you with your inheritance to say that. It's a lot more than a few quid to me."

Sarah heard the floorboard on the landing creak. "Jonathon, I'll pay your debts off, you don't need to do this. Please, help me."

"I'd love to, Sarah, but the amount he offered me is too much and will sort me out for a very long time. It's my future sorted."

Just as he finished speaking, Sarah felt a push against the door. She leaned back as hard as she could. As Tony pushed harder, she could feel her feet slipping across the carpet. With the next push, she used the impetus to launch herself at Jonathon, head down, like a rugby player taking out a prop forward. She screamed at the top of her voice as she hit him, and he fell back, smashing through the glass window. The breaking of the glass sounded like a small explosion in Sarah's ears.

Sarah and Jonathon fell through the broken window together, and as they passed through, she felt the icy cold rain through her blouse and then a searing pain in her thigh, which made her let out an ear-splitting scream. Jonathon hit the roof of the shed with a bone-crushing impact and Sarah landed on him before being catapulted onto the wet lawn. She tried to move, but she was badly winded by the impact, and began to crawl towards the table. Excruciating pain from her thigh prevented her from getting up, but she managed to grab the side of the table and pull it over towards her. Scrambling for her phone, she was struggling to unlock it because of the water on the screen. She tried to press speed dial for Officer Jennings, but Tony kicked the phone out of her hand.

"You've ruined my plan, Sarah. You were supposed to fall down the stairs and break your neck, and your fire would accidentally light the rug, setting the whole place alight. The police would find your charred remains, with a couple of bottles of wine in your system. Then I'd buy the farm cheap, because the main building was destroyed in the fire and Bob, as they say, is your uncle."

Sarah kicked out at him. "You sick, twisted bastard, I saw the whole thing. You, Terence and Lenny at the lake house. I watched you hit him with the rod and then leave him in the lake to drown. Now you've turned Jonathon against me. He was a good man, and a good friend."

"Sarah, dear Sarah. Lenny should never have mentioned the car, he panicked after you visited him. I had to put a bit of pressure on him to stop him from cracking and offer him a few quid more; and your lover boy, Jonathon, was a weak little man, he was easy to bring in. You killing him saves me from doing it. He actually believed that I was going to pay him, the pathetic little moron. He was going in the fire with you." He knelt down next to her and looked at her thigh. "Does it hurt?"

As he said it, he grabbed the shard of glass and began to twist it in her leg. Sarah let out an almighty scream and lashed out, scratching him across his face.

"Bitch! This new plan is even better than the original. You and Jonathon had a fight and fell through the window, which means the house is still intact."

He turned to look around, picking up a large shard of glass from the lawn and putting the point against the side of Sarah's neck. "This is going to hurt, but hopefully not for too long. Depends how quickly you bleed out."

As he started to apply pressure on her neck, she heard a crunching thud and watched as Tony slowly fell to the ground next to her. The rain was blinding her vision and it took a few seconds for her to focus. Stood over him was Jonathon with a broken piece of timber. She could hear the gurgling sound of Tony trying to breathe and turned to look at him. His eyes rolled back in his head, blood seeping from his ear and mouth on to the lawn, diluted by the rain, which made it look like a tiny, red river.

Sarah looked back at Jonathon as he lifted the weapon to strike. She cowered, pulling her arms up over her face, readying herself for the blow. There was another bone-crunching thud, but Sarah didn't feel any pain. She opened her eyes to see that he'd hit Tony again, before falling to his knees next to her.

His body limp and looking a pitiful shell of his former self, he muttered, "I'm so sorry, Sarah, please forgive me."

She hadn't realised that during Jonathon's assault on Tony, the glass had pierced her neck. She began to fade slowly into unconsciousness, but as she did, she could see other people in the garden. "Dad, is that you?"

Finding herself in the painting again, she was now standing just before the bridge. The smells and the colours were more powerful than ever before, and she saw the vapour leave her mouth with every breath. She looked around and her dad was standing beside her. He linked her arm as they walked over the bridge and into the forest without saying a word, until they finally reached the clearing.

He turned to her and gave her a kiss on her cheek. "This isn't your time, my love. You have a lot more to do with your life." Then she watched as he walked across the clearing and faded into the mist. Just as he started to disappear, he met with Sarah's mother, who linked her arm through his, blew Sarah a kiss, and smiled.

Sarah's eyes fill with tears. *You're both at peace now.*

Opening her eyes, she saw bright lights and a nurse leaning over her. "I'm not dead, then?"

The nurse gave her a huge smile. "No, Sarah, you're very much alive. The police are here; do you feel up to seeing them?"

She nodded and the nurse beckoned for Officer Jennings to come over. She sat down at the foot of the bed. "How are you feeling?"

Sarah puffed out her cheeks. "I'm fine," she replied. "What's happened to Tony and Jonathon."

"I heard the whole thing over the phone, including Tony's full confession. Officers are at Lenny's as we speak, arresting him. Tony is in hospital and will hopefully recover so that we can get true justice for your dad, and Jonathon is in the cells awaiting a court date. He asked to speak to you and asked me to pass on this letter."

"What about Terence?"

"We're trying to track him down, but he'll be arrested soon enough."

Officer Jennings patted Sarah on the shoulder gently and began to walk out. "We'll have a proper chat tomorrow. See you then."

Sarah laid back on her bed and opened the letter from Jonathon.

I'm sorry, you were a great friend and I've lost the chance for us to be more. I hope you can find it in your heart forgive me. Love, Jonny Boy.

CHAPTER
TWENTY-FIVE:

S arah arrived home on crutches; the house was cold and felt extremely empty.

Looking out of the kitchen window her garden looked like a scene from CSI. There was police tape and evidence markers everywhere. She was dreading going up to the bedroom to see what carnage was left up there. Before doing anything, though, she put the kettle on and settled herself down with a cup of tea.

Officer Jennings had said that she'd call in to check on her when she finished her shift around two o'clock, which gave her an hour or so to clean up.

At two-thirty, there was a knock at the door and Sarah opened it expecting the officer. But when she opened it a shiver ran through her, as standing in front of her with a rabid look on his face and a shotgun in his hand was Terence.

He barged in through the door pushing Sarah to the ground. "My brother is dead and it's your fault."

Shocked, and frightened, Sarah watched as he stood menacingly. "Terence?" she said, "he's not dead, he's in hospital. It was just a bang on the head, he'll be home soon."

She crawled back into the house, but as she crossed the threshold, Terence put his sturdy boot on her thigh. "You're lying," he growled.

She let out a scream and tried to push him away and through gritted teeth, fighting the excruciating pain, she managed to speak. "I'll prove it to you, just let me call the hospital, I'll get them to put him on the phone."

"You're lying again, you think I'm stupid. He's dead."

"Honestly, Terence, I promise you, he's not dead. Let me call the hospital and you can speak to him."

He moved his boot and she managed to stand, then picked up her phone and dialed the number. "Hello, is that the hospital? It's Sarah Pennington. I need to speak to Tony Culshaw, it's urgent."

A minute later, Sarah ended the call and looked back at Terence, his expression still of anger as he continued to hold the gun threateningly. "Terrence, I need to sit down. You can wait inside with me, if you like?" she said, hoping her calm approach might soften him and encourage him to take pity on her.

She took a seat on the settee while Terence still stood, leering over her. With in a couple of minutes, she saw a police car pull up through the side window behind him, but rather than alert him to their presence, she kept talking to him, trying to make sure his attention stayed on her.

One officer circled around the back while Officer Jennings went to the front door and opened it.

"Sarah, are you in here?" she called.

Terence turned towards the door and gestured with the gun for her to enter. "You need to put the gun down, Terry. You know me, I'm Lesley from the police liaison team."

"Come in and sit next to her," he gestured, brandishing the gun and pointing it towards Sarah. "If Tony doesn't call soon, I'll shoot her, then I'll give it ten more minutes before I shoot you. You should have stayed away."

It was as he finished speaking, the painting on the wall behind him suddenly fell, hitting him on the back. The shock of the impact made him spin around and involuntarily pull the trigger. There was an ear-piercing bang as the gun went off, followed by a second bang, and he fell to the floor holding his chest.

The second officer had shot him.

Sarah turned to Jennings, tears streaming down her face, but a feeling of huge relief now overwhelming her. "Thank you so much," she said. I was so scared he would say something when he couldn't hear who I was talking to on the phone. I was terrified he'd make me put it on loud speaker."

"It's over now," she said, taking hold of Sarah's hand. "We know Terry from old, he's had a history of being caught with guns. He's never used one, but I brought an armed officer just in case."

The ambulance arrived soon after and strapped Terrence onto a stretcher then loaded him inside.

"I'll stay with you for a while," Jennings said. "Shall I make some tea?"

"Thanks, I'd like that. Do you think Terence will by okay?"

Jennings offered Sarah a smile and shook her head. "No," she said, "he's gone."

Officer Jennings stayed for another hour then left. Sarah was exhausted, but glad it was over, and she went to her painting and picked it up, leaning it against the mantle and looking at it, this time with affection.

"Thank you, Dad," she said. "I know you and Mum are with me. I love you both."

Then the turned it around in her hands to look for the position of the fittings in order to attach it back to wall and just caught sight of some writing in the corner, fine black paint that read:

'A Bridge to Somewhere' 17th February 2008.

She smiled and hung it back up, taking a few steps back and admiring the image that she would never again refer to as 'The Nowhere Man'.

ACKNOWLEDGEMENTS

The first, and most important person I need to thank is my beautiful wife, Tracey. She read early drafts of my first book, Twilight Cruise and helped with the storyline, and then encouraged me to write The Nowhere Man. Thank you, Trace xx

I should also thank a very good friend of Tracey's for reading The Nowhere Man at first draft and giving me feedback. Thank you, Dawn.

A massive thank you to my editor, Kathryn Hall, who also helped with the cover design. Without her, The Nowhere Man would still be a file on my computer.

Finally, a big thank you to family, friends, and work colleagues, who read Twilight Cruise and gave me the push I needed to carry on with further books.

OTHER BOOKS

TWILIGHT CRUISE

A cruise for the elderly takes Mary and her husband Eddie on a wonderful journey on a beautiful ship, which transports them through the memories of a lifetime.

Dancing through the decades, wearing the clothes of their youth and reliving days gone by until an unexpected twist brings Mary back to reality.

Twilight Cruise will have you laughing out loud and reaching for the tissues throughout, with a twist to floor the strongest of hearts.

Winner of the TaleFlick Road to Development competition 2021, Twilight Cruise is currently being optioned for film/TV by Hollywood producer Uri Singer.

Printed in Great Britain
by Amazon

10540223R00093